JANUARY 2024 - ISSUE 208

FICTION

NON-FICTION

Neil Clarke: Publisher/Editor-in-Chief
Sean Wallace: Editor
Kate Baker: Non-Fiction Editor/Podcast Director

Clarkesworld Magazine (ISSN: 1937-7843) • Issue 208 • January 2024

clarkesworldmagazine.com

Nothing of Value

AIMEE OGDEN

For anyone who's used the Skip system to travel more than once or twice, delays are simply part of the process. The one following my transit to Olympus lasts longer than most. I pass the time by looking for a way to bend the causative incident behind the delay into a funny story to tell you when I see you. An icebreaker to crash through the rime of the last nine years. God, has it really been that long? Graduation feels like it was just yesterday; freshman orientation at Western Dome Technical University two weeks ago at most.

A little over twelve hours ago, I was a completely different set of similarly arranged atoms fifty light-minutes away. Time is relative.

At least the wait is more comfortable than it used to be, in the early days. The printing room where I'm locked down looks new, or at least recently updated. It's warm, and the condensation clinging to my skin after the printing process evaporates quickly. There's even a clothing printer already calibrated to the specs from my Scanometric; a far cry from stumbling out of the printer wet and shivering after my first transit down to Earth, only to have to fumble my way into a one-size-fits-most paper jumpsuit. Transit has come such a long way since we were kids, though I doubt you're aware of that, you dear old Luddite.

At my input, the printer doles out a pair of chloroskin trousers and a gray linen shirt. Fashion has to have changed since we were college kids, but I can deal with going for a sort of offbeat retro look. By the time I've dressed, but before I've figured out how to manufacture a cute anecdote out of the wait, the lockdown ends: the lights shift from amber to yellow-white, the alarm drifts down-key and out of the range of human hearing. All clear, and the door clicks to let me know it's unlocked.

This time, I'm not going to let cowardice win. Not cowardice—*inertia*. It's been too long. I need to see you. Hold you. You'd never be the first one to say it, but I think it must be the same for you.

It's not long before an attendant appears at the window to ask me how I found my trip. "Easy as falling asleep," I say, like I always do, and she humors me with a polite laugh, like the attendants always do, before starting the diagnostic scan on my print job.

I take a detour through the city as I come out of the transit station; it's not as if you're expecting me at a certain time anyway. The station isn't the only thing that's changed. The bohemian academic Mars of our youth has been swept aside and buried under a fresh layer of garish red-and-blue paint. When I turn toward downtown on Meridian 37, the dorm towers where we used to live are gone—no more baleful gaps to show where stolen solar panels once hung. Half a dozen kids run and scream in the open space left behind, kicking up clouds of dirt and crumbs as they go. That must be a corporate-chain grocery store in the abandoned corner of space we used to sneak into. For a few hours, worries about exams and indentures fell out of sight, where we would drink liquor we weren't supposed to have (and sometimes fuck, when our roommates couldn't take a hint). Across the way, a public toilet occupies the spot where a coffee cart always stood.

Your ID tag autocompletes when I start to pull it up in the habitat's datascape, as if the habitat itself were trying to hurry me along. A shudder of relief shakes my shoulders: your address is hidden, but at least I know now for certain that you *are* still here somewhere.

Your expression in the photo attached to your account is neutral. Is your hair gray beneath your headband? Are those lines from worry, or laughter? We used to laugh; you used to worry.

Your public messaging is unlocked. Maybe I should have put more effort into figuring out what to say. I don't have a funny story to share; I don't even have a way to glibly say: hey, remember that pact we made when we were young and stupid and in love? *Meet me at our spot*, I message, and regret it as soon as I've hit send. But it's too late to take it back now, and sometimes simple and straightforward is the best choice.

We were just freshmen when Skip2 deployed its first functional prototypes.

Since the Ship of Theseus had now been thoroughly sunk, we riddled each other with exactly the same questions that nerdy teenagers have been asking since the idea of teleportation first popped into a science fiction writer's head. If you could hack your Scanometric, what would you change? Giving yourself two more inches of height, a bigger dick. Erase scars or clear the dust-scarring from lungs. *I want freckles*, you said. *Not the dura-ink kind. Real ones.*

How about this: would you peek at someone else's Scanometric if you could? What if a technical error happened and the shell didn't get recycled at the exit facility, so there were two of you walking around the universe—would you fuck yourself, and if so, would that be incest or masturbation?

Don't say shell, you would complain. *Don't say recycling.*

It was all theoretical at that point anyway. We were broke college kids, saving printer rations to trade for booze. Those first trips cost *years*' worth of UBI. Still, we talked about where we would go, if we could be there and back in the blink of an eye. Europa. Ottawa, to visit your gran. Uranus, I suggested, barely suppressing a smirk, and we both snickered like naughty schoolkids.

At some point, around fourth semester exams, I noticed two things: transit had gotten a lot cheaper, and you'd stopped laughing along.

Those were tough exams. Both of us were struggling, watching our scores slink downward. Chances to slip away to the empty building got fewer and farther between; chances to slam a bottle of cheap wine and crack philosophical dwindled to nothing. I think we both saw our paths diverging, too. Which was why it was so important to make sure they crossed again, someday.

Even if that day was very far. You could hop across the Settlements by then, as fast as your information could hurtle through the space in between. (Well. *You and I* couldn't. Some people could.) But no one had invented a way to teleport a person through time. And I know no one ever will, at least not in our lifetimes. Because otherwise, the version of me that prints back into a fresh new body in Olympus would have taken a moment to pop back into the past and tell our college selves: *hey, look, it's going to be a while, but no one has to say goodbye for good, okay?*

Our spot has changed, too. It's not an awkwardly sized coffee shop-slash-sushi joint anymore, which is sad, and also probably for the best. That was a combination from hell; it's not as if there's aquaculture on Mars, so that "fresh fish" was, at best, sitting in an interplanetary transit box for four, five days. We both got food poisoning at least once. But studying for exams was hell anyway; synthetic coffee and week-old shrimp tempura at least upgraded us to one of the higher circles. We were nineteen, so probably the one Dante reserved for Lust.

At some point, they sold the building and knocked down the wall in between that weirdly shaped corner shop and the tech repair place next door. Now the whole thing is occupied by an unremarkable chip shop. It smells like old oil, and so will I, I'm sure, before I leave.

I've never made it this far before. Five times now I've come back to Mars, and five times I've turned right back around and printed back out on Venus. Without seeing you, without saying a word. Without you ever knowing I was here. Without me ever knowing I was here, except for the fact that I was reprinting back in Gioconda—I've never stayed long enough to even bother making a new Scanometric. And God knows you'd never come meet me there; not if it means using the transit. It's been too long. That's my fault—mostly—but it doesn't make it untrue.

This time it's going to be different. This time I'm moving too fast, with too much purpose, to be overcome by the inertia of cowardice.

The closest thing to where "our" booth stood is a six-top table. It's already taken by a young parent, a baby, and, based on the flavor of *goo-goo-ga-ga* cooing coming out of the last occupant's mouth, the baby's grandparent. I stand around, waiting, in case they're on the verge of finishing up, but the baby is busy squashing cold fries in its fingers and the adults are busy thinking this is the cutest and best thing any living being has ever done. I bet that baby has never developed a microbe with a novel sulfur dioxide metabolic pathway.

The parent gives me an annoyed look and stretches out, feet plopping onto the chair opposite. I roll my eyes and plug an order into the kiosk's greasy buttons, choosing a different table—still within view of the six-top, although there's a partial wall in between to make me feel a little less like I'm looming—to sit at and wait. You might be at work or sleeping; who knows what shift you're on? The chip shop says it's open twenty-four hours, and I don't mind waiting. Besides, I'm always hungry after a fresh printing.

The fries aren't that good—some people say they can taste the difference between printed potatoes and off-worlded ones, but I think these are just undercooked—and the best thing that can be said about the beer is that it's cold. My bladder fills before my stomach does, so I leave my room-temperature fries on the table to find the nearest public washroom on the street nearby. It's free to use, which is a pleasant surprise—the alleys behind this shop always smelled a lot worse, back in our days. I check my overlay as I walk back to the chip shop, scanning my messages with a backdrop of passersby and samey-samey buildings, giving me a clear, and boring, education on modern Martian architecture. No reply yet from you. I double-check my uplink to make sure I'm still on the local 'scape, but my connection says it's strong. I give myself a hundred reasons for your silence: you're at work, you're sleeping, you've turned your overlay off so you can dance uninterrupted to that awful neogrunge lithocore band you loved so much. Big Berry Bronze, was that their name? I try to call it up from the 'scape and get a listing of where in Olympus I can buy imported fresh fruit from Earth or the Martian agriculture rings. It distracts me enough that I almost brush right past you, peering in through the front window of the chip shop.

"Hey," I say, because what else is there to say, and for bonus triteness I add: "Been a while."

You startle as you turn from the window. For a moment we stand awkwardly, evaluating the right mode of greeting for an absence this long. Our arms shift stiffly, not quite folding into a hug; we end up clasping—but not quite shaking—hands in the space between us. "Look at you," you say, and let go of my hand. "You look the same as ever."

"Well, I got older!" Though technically I did spring for the de-aging protocol to be applied to a few of my Scanometrics over the years. Vanity comes for us all, in the end. "You grew your hair long. I like it."

"I really thought after last time, I wouldn't see you again," you say, and even though it's been years, I'm still not ready to see you cry again, so I usher you inside before you can start: toward mushy fries and watery Martian beer and a corner table where we can talk, just you and me and the here-and-now. A river of time has flowed between us, but rivers leave silt behind, and if there's not enough here to walk across, I'll risk floundering to try.

The assignment to Vitruvius would have paid off my student indenture in one go, which is the only reason I was considering it at all. But when I came to you with my research—the medtech jobs that would be available to you on Venus, the comfortable corporate housing where we could live almost rent-free, even a selection of cute coffee shops near the new development sector—you laughed in my face. *They want you on Monday*, you said to me. *Are you fucking kidding me?*

It didn't bother me, I reminded you, and you reminded me back that it bothered the fuck out of you.

This isn't even a question, you said. *The whistleblowers were pretty clear on that point. You will literally die. It will literally kill you.*

I felt like "whistleblowers" was a pretty lofty title to attach to the Skip2 engineers who changed their mind ex post facto. A few of them had been in the news, wailing about what they had specifically designed their product to do. They had plenty of time to wail and gnash their teeth and rend their garments and whatever else you do in that kind of situation; by that point, the drama had made them thoroughly unemployable, even to companies that weren't covered by Skip2's noncompete clause. And anyone with even a Group Three science education knew you couldn't actually shoot a human being's worth of matter across the solar system in a matter of minutes.

But you could send *information* about how to assemble that same amount of matter.

A version of me would die, I argued. But then a version would live, too, and nothing of value was actually lost. An exact copy with the same feelings and memories, the same bad habits, and the same favorite coffee cup. Everyone was doing it—they wouldn't be, if it wasn't totally fine. The corporations would have shut it down so they wouldn't get sued. The International Supervisory Board review had said that there was nothing unsafe or unreasonable about Skip2 travel.

Maybe you should do it, you said to me, and because you always got a little mean when we fought you added: *the universe could do with one fewer version of you.*

It took me a few days to apologize to you. It took me a few days to decide whether I wanted to. But I knew you would never apologize first. *You wouldn't really have done it, would you?* you asked, and you sounded so relieved I could only tell you: no, of course not, I would never.

You order a filled roll from the kiosk—"Terrible fries, but they have an agreement with the bakery on the row behind," you explain—and we find two seats in a quiet corner of the chip shop. While you pick at the roll, you dole out polite questions about my work: do I have my own office yet, how is the artificial weather this time of year, did I like working on the bioforming project for the new habitat on Venus?

I hand back answers: no; fine, but a little too warm for my taste; and I'm surprised that you've kept up with the news from Gioconda enough to know about the bioforming project. That makes you laugh, and you look down at your roll as you tear a new strip off the side.

The pause gives me a chance to steer the conversation for a while. "Enough about me and my microbes. How have things been here?"

You set down the piece of roll without eating it. "With me, or with Mars?"

"Both."

"Good."

I wait, and you concede, rattling off information as if it's a speech you've memorized. "It was pretty wild there for a while, but it's been a quiet four or five years now. Last month I finished a two-year term on the Citizen's Council; I liked it, but it took too much of my time, especially during interlocutive assessment season."

"Interlocutive assessment?" I interrupt. "You're not interlocuting with your immunonanoparticles, I assume?"

"No. I haven't touched an INP node for six years." You still sound as if you're reading from an encyclopedia entry about your life. "I work in a crèche now, with the filter class that's headed into the tech track of underschool."

"A crèche!" My incredulity would be easy to mistake for outrage. I rein it in, so you don't get the wrong idea. "But—what about your student indenture contract? You'd still owe another year to the university's sponsor corporations."

"I see you *haven't* been keeping up with the news from Mars."

"Work keeps me busy." And, I don't add, it's not as if I would have expected to see your name in a Martian news report, Mx. Citizen Councilor.

"Of course." You look sideways, out the chip shop window. It's quiet out on the corridor, hardly anyone hurrying this way or that. There's a woman loitering on the bench attached to the front of the housing block across the corridor, and a bored-looking cleaning tech wiping down windows on the same building. "Then you missed reading about the riots six years ago. Most of the buildings in this sector were destroyed. We own the university now—all of us here—and there's no more indenture."

"Wow," I say and can't help adding cheekily: "Too bad about Maki-n-Mocha, though."

That gets me about half a smile. I remember my partially assembled anecdote and fumble to put it together on the fly. "The transit station is nicer these days, too. I almost didn't mind hanging out in the printing room waiting around for an attendant to clear my print."

Your smile retracts. "You mean because of the lockdown? I saw it on the 'scape."

"They caught the shell pretty fast—only twenty minutes or so before they could get it back into the recycler. 'Lockdown' is a strong word for twenty minutes." I snort. "That's barely enough time for a post-print stretch to make sure all my parts came through right."

"Don't," you say. "Don't say 'shell.'" And you certainly don't laugh. Too late, I remember how you stopped laughing along.

It was a few years before the prices came down. A few years of drudgery, the stench and boredom of wastewater microbial health. I watched the days of my indenture tick by one at a time. And one day, I took a day off work and Ported to Earth for an afternoon.

Nowhere special: the Chicago hub, because it was cheaper than the other options I looked at, and because I'd had ancestors from Indiana (where there wasn't a printing hub yet). I wandered around under a sky full of low, gray clouds that felt enough like a dome that I didn't get agoraphobic, I ate a veggie hot dog, I ogled some buildings that would have looked like toys next to Olympus Mons. I Ported back home before dinnertime.

Working at the hospital kept you busy, and you were living on the other side of the dome by then. We met in the middle for bad sushi and decaf coffee, and I didn't say anything to you about how I'd spent my day. As far as you could see, hear, smell, taste, feel, it was still me. It's always been me.

"Let's just fast-forward through this part this time." When you speak again, you sound defensive, like you've deviated from whatever encyclopedic script you've been working from. "I started working in the crèche because of Jani," you say, dropping the wreckage of your bread roll onto the plate. "That's my partner Emilian's son."

You're watching my reaction. I don't know what you see, but I know what it feels like: my throat tight and my chest expanding with the breath I can't release. My hands are cold and my face too hot. "You never told me," I say, when I can speak again. "That you had a partner and a kid. You never said anything."

Your face pulls tight, and your eyes are cold. You never used to look at me like that, even when we fought. "Two partners, actually."

"But—you're mono!" You shrug noncommittally, and I don't even try to bite off the next words before they can leave my mouth. "Are they both *puritans* like you?"

"Voula used the transit a couple of times, early on, before she decided she didn't like it." Your fingers push breadcrumbs around, leaving obscure patterns. "Can we just jump to the end of this already?"

"We made a pact—we promised each other!"

"*There* we go." Under your palm, the crumbs mash together. "Like I tell you every time you bring that up: I was nineteen. I was drunk, and so were you. *Nineteen and drunk is not a binding vow.*"

The broken pieces of the promise carve up the space between us into a twisted labyrinth. I'm lost, and I can't see the way out. "You thought transit would change me," I say. "You're the one who's different. A whole different flavor of *asshole*. You could have at least said something! Told me you'd moved on. Walked back everything we promised each other instead of waiting for me to show up and make a fool of myself."

I regret the anger as soon as it's too late to rein it in. But the look you throw at me projects pity more than hurt. "I don't know why I do this to myself," you say, pushing back from the table. When you look out the window, I follow your gaze again. The woman on the bench has stood up, and she's looking at the chip shop. On a hunch, I run a search on the datascape: Voula, with your surname appended. The photo on the ID profile that shows up matches the face outside. So that's how it is. "I have to go. See you next time, I guess. Or not."

"Or not," I echo. I'm left to resort to borrowing your words; none of mine are up to the task right now. You sweep past me without acknowledgment. You don't stop to collect the woman—Voula—but she hurries in your wake, reaching for your hand. You vanish around the curve of the corridor before I can see if you let her take it.

By the time we had our final fight, we'd put aside philosophical arguments. It was all: *you'll die if you do it; do you want to die*? And I'd say, no, I want to *live*, and how am I supposed to do that while I'm stuck in here in this indenture? *Living in a company town isn't much of an improvement.* But we couldn't know, not really, unless we tried something different. *Then fucking go*, you said, because you lived for the last word, and there was nothing, really, left to say after that anyway.

So I did. I went. To Luna, first, even if I was just doing wastewater microbial health there, too, and it wasn't paying off my indenture any faster. The really cushy jobs had already been sucked up fast, when people were still cautious and curious about the transit—when you still had to offer a lot of cash to get people into a Skip station. At least it was something else, somewhere else. At least I was trying. The coffee shops in Archimedes Two sucked, though, and better assignments came after that. I did land at Vitruvius, eventually, for a six-month long temp gig; Sattva Station and Europa and the Jovian Stratospheric Array and, finally, Gioconda. It's nice there. Reminds me of Olympus ten years ago. I paid off my indenture last year, fifteen months ahead of schedule.

And if I get tired of it there, it's easy enough to keep moving. Doesn't matter how deep the roots have grown, as long as you're within travel distance of any Skip station. You can just pick up and move on, start fresh: just you and none of the trappings. All that stuff is just fluff. Decoration. The core, everything you really need—that stays the same wherever you go.

Or maybe I should say: wherever *I* go.

• • •

When you leave, I'm the last one in the chip shop, except for a cleaning drone that's stuck wiping the same corner of floor between two tables. Voula's profile is already up in my overlay; from there, it's easy enough to find Emilian's. The kid's profile is locked down, of course, but I could send a message to either of your spouses, or both. I could say . . . what? "To the victor go the spoils." "Good luck—you're going to need it." After a few abortive efforts, I delete everything I've written, which isn't much.

There's a line under the Unplanned Itineraries sign, when I get back to the station, a dozen other last-minute travelers. They wear a range of expressions: bored, impatient, nervous, excited. I work on my travel documentation in my overlay while I wait, uploading the finished form as soon as I can. When an attendant comes to collect me from the back of the line, the other travelers give me sour looks. They probably don't know that you can get expedited recycling if you're willing to skip the outbound data collection.

"Reason for Scanometric deferral?" the attendant asks, a tedious legal requirement, as I'm ushered into the first available recycling pod. The floor is still damp, and it smells like the processing chemicals leftover from the pod's previous use.

I shrug out of the clothes I printed earlier and hand them back to her for separate processing. "Didn't learn anything of value during my stay."

"Thank you," says the attendant, flashing a comforting smile. I wonder if they always do that, on this end of transit. No way to know, and honestly, no reason to care. My previous Scanometric is racing to Gioconda, and I'll meet it there; and you'll stay here, where you've always been. Whoever you are now. I know who I am, with or without you.

The attendant closes the pod door, and I'm ready to go. I've always been ready.

For anyone who's used the Skip system to travel more than once or twice, delays are simply part of the process. At least the one following my transit to Olympus is a short one: the clothing printer jams before I can get more than a sleeve out of it. While the attendant fiddles with the printer, I look for ways to turn all of this into a joke about modern Martian fashion, something to make you laugh when I see you again. I'm ready to hear your laugh again, after ten years. God, has it really been that long?

ABOUT THE AUTHOR

Aimee Ogden is an American werewolf in the Netherlands. Her debut novella, *Sun-Daughters, Sea-Daughters* was a Nebula Award finalist, and her short fiction has also appeared in publications such as *Lightspeed, Beneath Ceaseless Skies,* and *Strange Horizons,* as well as previously in *Clarkesworld.* She also co-edits *Translunar Travelers Lounge,* a magazine of fun and optimistic speculative fiction.

Down the Waterfall

CÉCILE CRISTOFARI

On nights when the time traveler's body has knitted enough of itself back up, she remembers what it feels like to sleep like a human. She abandons herself to a sluggishness she knows will come without pain, tastes the relief of no longer watching out for lethal dangers hidden in every thought. She dreams, and she forgets.

If she was not too exhausted to remember, she would wake up clinging to the fading image of a face gazing at her across a curtain of water. A smile; kind, sharp eyes holding hers through the blur; a hand outstretched, so close to her she could reach out and hold it, if not for the waterfall barreling down between them.

The time traveler isn't a time traveler yet. She's a student, with an overflowing mind and far too little time to put all her dreams to the test. When her thoughts grow crowded, she untangles them in a roadside café, away from the city, at the edge of a hamlet trapped between tall rocks and forbidding crevices.

She sits there now, twisting her spoon in her coffee cup. He's sitting across from her, and smiles at something she's just said.

"A waterfall. That's a poetic way to put it," he says.

He's teasing her. She's a physicist whose brain tends to work faster than her tongue. He's the poet, one she admires—he's her friend, too. She smiles back.

"Perhaps. Put it this way: what do you get if you stop a waterfall from moving?"

He nods, slightly, for her to go on.

"You don't get a still waterfall," she says. "You get nothing. A waterfall isn't just water. It's movement. The bedrock is needed, and the water, of course. But it's only with motion that it starts to exist."

"And in your analogy, we are . . . ?"

"The waterfall itself," she says.

He nods again. She thinks he really does understand. The nature of time is hard to wrap words around; emotions are an easier way to understand it. She takes a sip from her coffee. It's bitter and unsubtle, but they both come here for the view, not the drinks. She gazes at the brook flowing at the bottom of the valley, nearly dried-up in this season. The twisted pines clinging to blocks of white limestone, higher up in the mountain, make do with sheer will and a few raindrops a year.

She glances at him, hoping he doesn't see her do that. The sun throws stark shadows on his face. His expression is the thoughtful, gentle one she likes more than she ought to.

"So, traveling in time . . . " he prompts again, sensing that her thoughts have gone astray.

"Should be impossible, yes. At least by the laws of physics as we understand them. Disturb the movement, and you don't exist anymore. But then . . . suppose there might be something in us that is not bound by the laws of physics. Something we haven't yet accounted for, precisely because the current equations cannot make sense of it."

"Something metaphysical?"

"That's the hypothesis, yes."

He smiles, again. Touches her hand.

"Whether it works or not, you've come up with a beautiful thought," he says.

Her smile wavers. As much as she enjoys those meetings, she finds herself unnerved, at times, when strands of her mind wander in directions she doesn't mean to explore—another life, another rivulet of time, where this friendship of theirs would have taken a different form. She thinks of her husband and takes another sip of her coffee.

The time traveler hugs her daughter, kisses her husband, makes a chipper joke, then, after ascertaining that they've left the house, collapses in an armchair with her head lolling to the side.

She had imagined the pain, in an abstract way. She had devised a kill switch, just in case. What she had not planned for was the way the microorganisms would disrupt motor control, so that when the agony became unbearable, she was unable to get her muscles to press the button. She has gone through the ordeal, pain intense enough to shut her body down.

Which had been the point all along, all things considered.

She flexes her hands, briefly surprised that they have recovered normal feeling and reaction. She takes deep breaths.

The realization that the machine worked will overwhelm her, probably, when her body has taken a little time to convince itself that it really is still alive. She stands up. Her legs shake, only a little now. She walks to the bookshelves. Her eyes fall on a poetry collection, and her heart tightens a little.

Her last message to him sits on her phone undeleted. *Sorry I couldn't make it to your reading.* There was no answer. It would have annoyed him, she thinks. She hopes it did; she doesn't want to think that her presence mattered too little to him for her absence to disappoint.

Theories focused on speed have established it: traveling fast enough for time to become a malleable entity would require the sort of power that could end the life of a star. Enough speed to plunge into darkness, the absolute unknown.

It is her poet friend who remarks one day that the darkness will engulf every soul eventually; every life will lose the light of its star, and the world will continue, nonetheless. He says it like a joke, and she answers with a wry smile. Poetry, again.

As she gazes at the golden foam vanishing on the top of her coffee cup, however, her mind stops moving. Every life, every star. No superluminal speed, only a moment when time becomes meaningless, when what was suddenly isn't, a quantic change no one has so far managed to measure.

"Unless . . . " she begins.

"Unless?"

"Unless we are looking at an event where the laws of physics don't apply," she says.

She raises a finger. Her mind is moving faster, or perhaps sinking deeper. Where the laws of physics don't apply. Where there is no need for speed, and therefore for power. One single moment when the mind breaks free of time, of physics. If that moment could be harnessed somehow . . .

He waits. She is aware that he's looking at her. Not staring; he'll never break propriety with her. Her heart accelerates, a little.

Not for the first time, she wonders whether the meandering stream of time has truly filled the void with an infinity of branching worlds, or if that concept hovers between wishful thinking and philosophical experiment. Not for the first time, the thought makes her uncomfortable, and she shakes free of it.

"Remind me when they've scheduled your reading?" she says.

"A month from now. Plenty of time."

His latest collection already sits on her bookshelf. Sometimes at night, she opens it in random places, and hears his deep, mesmerizing voice reading the lines. When some of the more eager of the university's students extended an invitation to read his poems as part of a student conference, he joked about it, but she could sense how pleased he was, nonetheless. She rarely enjoys student talks but promised to come anyway.

When they part, the back of her mind still attempts to wrap itself around whatever could lie outside the laws of the physical world, and what "power" could mean there. It's like having an obstinate creature inside her, groping and twisting itself around her own ignorance, never relenting until it's burst open.

It is a simple question of perception, she explains (remembers explaining).

For a drop of water falling, there is no escaping the momentum. There is only forward and downward.

For an outside observer, there is a blur of foam bouncing over rocks, ever-changing, but constant. You could train your eye to follow individual drops of water, or you could travel up and down the stream, with no limit to what you could see but that of your patience.

What happens when the waterfall runs out of water? someone says, to annoy you or to play with you—there are many someones *over the course of your life. You raise an eyebrow (a playful one, or a politely impatient one, it depends). You've just defined entropy, you reply, and move on.*

From the outside, her life will stare at her, address her like an old friend. She will be terrified to see herself like this, the first time. It's not just the sense of dissociation. It's the sight of her timeline, splayed there, pinned there, ready for dissection. As if she had died and—

She *has*. That is exactly the point.

There's a knock at the door.

"Mummy?"

She starts so violently she thinks she's back in the machine, fighting the pull of the microorganisms that devour her from the inside out.

"Mummy, I've made biscuits," the little voice says again.

It's tiny, hesitant, fearful, even. It breaks her heart.

She ignores the trembling in her legs and runs to the door. Her daughter stands there, eyes wide open, not quite smiling. She holds a tray of colorful things that look misshapen and delicious.

The time traveler beams at her daughter. She picks up the tray, sets it on the ground, then hugs her with love that she now knows neither passing years nor diverging timelines will extinguish. She sits down on the ground, feels the flow of time catch up with her at last, sweeping her along, gently, lovingly.

The biscuits are filled with muddied swirls of food coloring where they haven't browned in the oven. They taste of hard, toasted flour. She devours them, while her daughter climbs into her lap and rests her head against her shoulder.

"Will you tell me a story tonight, Mum?"

The time traveler's heart sinks into itself. She's lost track of days while harnessed in her machine. She doesn't remember a time when her daughter felt she had to *ask* for a story.

"Of course I will," she says.

Sorry I couldn't make it to your reading, her memory supplies, unbidden.

She hugs her daughter harder.

The solution to time travel, as it happened, was indeed neither speed nor power.

The perception of a single entity, a single body and mind united and streaming through time together, was nothing more than a trick of the brain to avoid losing itself in a reality too complex to grasp in full. Boundaries were no more than concepts.

Cells replace themselves in a constant stream. So do the millions of organisms without which their unsuspecting host could not live. One life harbors countless others, with no more unity than that of fragments temporarily moving in the same direction. All it takes to awake to the perception of a single entity moving through time is a perfect state of balance, cells firing and shutting down in unison, an ecosystem given light.

All it takes to destroy that perception is for the ecosystem to fall apart. And she has found out how to do it. Millions of microorganisms permeating her body, inside and outside, taking it apart until it is on the brink of collapse—and then rebuilding it, one cell after the other, even as it is being destroyed.

She has found the place where a body can indefinitely remain on the edge of death. No longer alive to be trapped in the flow of time; just alive enough to understand what it is going through.

She knows there will be pain. She expects danger, though she is not overly worried. She has seen rats recover, run without faltering through the maze she had trained them to cross moments before. She cannot really imagine that she could watch herself from above and be unable to anchor herself again in her own body.

She steps inside the machine, activates the restraints. The microorganisms swarm her, invade her nose, her ears, her mouth.

She screams.

Here

Right here

Watch yourself

Watch us

Watch . . .

A little girl running on a dirt path, playing at chasing invisible aliens. You, before you knew what numbers were.

A hand fumbling with a ring, then sliding it on your finger. You were very young. You never regretted it.

Sleepless nights, sleepy days, reading, calculating, pondering. The spines of rats breaking under your hands, their bodies interchangeable, discarded after outliving their usefulness. The three that survived the first trials of the time machine, your hand hesitating for the first time, then putting them in a box, smuggling them out of the lab and gifting them to your daughter.

A little girl with eyes as large and deep as the sea. A love you didn't know the human mind was capable of.

A hand laid on yours as gently as a falling leaf. To you, the distracted, tongue-tied physicist, he said you had the soul of a poet. He was not mocking.

Lives intertwined, flowing, falling.

The night is dark, slightly chilly. They walk together through the city center. Bars are noisy, and one could comfortably read a book in the glare of the streetlights. She regrets the quiet of the restaurant they've just left.

She's explained about death, as best she could. Like Zeno's paradox: your final moments bring you closer and closer, but never quite reach it, time stretching out indefinitely before what was *you* no longer is. Like Zeno's paradox, it is a falsehood. Death will happen, eventually. The thread will break. What used to be *you* will no longer be relevant—unless one can stretch the moment forever. Unless there is a way for death to become a true asymptote, to extend the exact moment of passing until it becomes a state in itself, and no longer a single point in time.

She's explained about near-death experiences, and how she thinks they could be harnessed.

Then she's stopped talking. It's just as comfortable this way, walking side by side with a friend in too-bright streets, stretching the last of the evening as far as she can before they have to part ways.

"I imagine you'll be buried in your work for the next few weeks," her friend says, his tone light.

"Probably. I have the model, not the math. I'll need to convince the department to ask for extra funding, a couple of PhDs to help around." She sighs. "Sounds dreary, I know."

He pats her shoulder. She walks a little closer to him.

"I'll see you at the reading, then," he says, hugging her before he departs.

She looks back, once, at his receding figure, then walks home.

The pain was a pinprick short of unbearable the first time. That missing pinprick was all it took to convince her to go back, until she'd learned to anticipate it enough that it no longer scared her. The disorientation that followed was, in its own way, almost worse.

She now knows why human minds can only perceive the present moment. The jumble of perceptions, sensations, emotions she experiences when that limitation is lifted pins her in place, and she flails around, silently screaming, while the stream of time crashes and washes over her.

Swim, a desperate instinct says. She cannot. She braces herself, tumbles, feels for the bedrock. Somehow, though she has no body to assist her, what is left of her consciousness still perceives itself in terms of legs, chest, mouth. She gropes around. She senses cold, pressure like rushing water, and then, little by little, something solid under her feet, a firmness she can feel with her entire body.

Centimeter by centimeter, she begins to wade.

She's talked to journalists, a few times. Invariably, they've asked her if she believed that her theory would turn the laws of physics on their head. It won't, she says; she is not certain yet whether one can test it and survive. A few times, she joked that there were no *laws* in physics, since laws must be enforced, and she had yet to meet an enforcer. It created more discomfort than it was worth, and she focused on getting the next interviews done with quickly.

In the evenings she shared tea with her husband, only occasionally talking about work, resting on the sofa with her head on his shoulder, and then, later, commiserating about their joint exhaustion as soon as their baby had fallen asleep at last. When her daughter whimpered again, she nursed her and soothed her and sang half-formed words, part of her mind still wandering around possibilities. Whether, if she managed to dissociate herself from the flow of time, she would be able to see moments that should be inaccessible to her but come no closer than an observer peering through a window; or whether she would manage to travel there for good.

Then when her baby's head rested quietly at last on her chest, she touched her cheek to her hair, wrapped herself in her warmth and gentle scent and the sound of her breath, savored the moments she was gifted, and no longer thought about anything.

It is like grief: a part of you wades ahead, hit with the full force of the waterfall, gasping and sputtering and grasping at the rocks that jut out without really knowing what they are. The other observes, curious, a bit relieved to feel nothing, a little underwhelmed.

When the two merge, it will feel like having your whole body fused into a tree through blunt force. But for now you wade, and you try to look, and you *are not convinced that you'll survive, though* I *am confident we will.*

You watch moments drift by, swift as fish. Some you recognize, some you almost do. There's no distance here, no memory filtering and deforming, and you're hit by strangeness, experiencing memories you thought would never fade and realizing how much they have, after all.

There are others wading or tumbling alongside you, and with a jolt, you realize that your intuition was right. Your machine mimics what happens to all minds as they die. The minds of the dying surround you, though they will never come back to tell of it.

You're overwhelmed by the certainty that you won't come back, either. From my vantage point, sitting in that bubble of quiet where it seems that nothing can reach me, I tell you that it is only natural. You're dying. Myriads of organisms are devouring your body, digesting it and regenerating it every moment. But I review the theory and find no fault in it; in fact, what we are seeing only confirms our most precise hypotheses. You have no reason to panic.

You grit your teeth and wade on. Then you open your eyes wide, choking. This is you, holding a book. This is your husband, smiling, though he looks a little uncertain. You've been reading that book a lot, he says, trying to keep it casual. You smile back, trying not to act guilty. It's just a poetry book. You were supposed to attend a reading of it, not so long ago.

You have no actual memory of that incident. You weren't ready for that little bit of pain to poke you. You hold on to the rock below. You once theorized that not everything is movement, and that the passing of time weathers a portion of reality into a slowly changing shape. This is what you are holding now. You try to look, but even from here, you cannot comprehend what is not in motion.

You keep searching.

*You—I—*her being jolts and solidifies again into one, and she rises and collapses on the ground. It worked. That's her first thought every time, as if surviving were not a given.

They've asked her to partner with a medical team. Her body needs to be monitored. She hasn't told her husband and daughter that. Instead, she's told them every test had come back all right.

As often as her strength can allow it, she climbs back into the machine, lets the microorganisms flood her steel coffin, and carries on looking.

She never stops. Copies of her machine are made; colleagues congratulate her on the income the patent has afforded her lab. There are talks of using her device in research, in law enforcement, ethical committees discussing every aspect she has not concerned herself with. None of this feels like it should matter to her.

She never stops, even now that she has done all the pioneering that could be expected of her, even when it becomes plain that her reassurances are not enough for her husband and daughter. She climbs into the coffin and tells herself that there is always more to learn.

And then she glides along the branching streams of her life.

You never remembered the moment when your now-husband's steps receded down the stairs, as he left home for the final time, taking a suitcase worth of belongings and a deep well of bitterness with him—or the moment when he came back, five days later, and you hugged him as the coffee burned in the espresso machine. Of course you don't remember. It never happened to you; that does not make it exist any less.

Parallel futures. But what you see in the falling waters of time is infinitely more complex, a web where the definition of existence *itself must be rewritten. What you are sensing is beyond words, beyond mathematics. Perhaps the microorganisms you entrusted your body to will evolve an understanding of it, eventually. Perhaps you could swim downstream and find out.*

This is what you are here for, after all, isn't it? Researching what happens up and down the stream?

• • •

"Isn't that what we write for?" he says, and his voice is gentle and uncertain.

She wonders what she would do if their hands were to touch as they walk. She doesn't think she would pull away. She would allow their fingers to entangle, and pretend it was an accident.

He has already picked another subject.

"What would it be to *you*, then? A sign that you've led a life worth living?"

"Flower shirts at my funeral," she replies, without really thinking.

He gazes at her, waits for her to go on, as he always does.

"I would want people to feel I wasn't the type of person they could possibly honor by wearing black," she says.

They walk in companionable silence after that. Close to one another, but their fingers never brush.

That one you remember. What you said, how you wondered for hours after that why the conversation had taken such a turn, how you walked back home and left him at the corner of the street leading to his hotel, and how his arms felt when you shared a hug.

Years raced past. Years are *racing past you even now—whatever* now *means here—and yet you can somehow grasp their substance. Extend a finger to touch them, feel them prickle your skin like ice-cold drops of water. You keep a steady footing. You wait.*

You stop breathing.

Not death, no.

You've found it.

You push your terror aside, and you dive.

You—I—we—

She steps inside.

For a moment she pushes through the overwhelm of perceptions

Fights the current

Chokes as moments slip from her grasp and this one too is about to escape her

Fights fights fights

And then

Perceptions assume the names of senses again and seeing becomes feeling and the overwhelm dies around her and she steps inside the flow and the flow becomes a door and she steps

Inside a room dotted with unassuming chairs and a modest crowd with their backs to her, not many people, though the numbers are far from embarrassing, for a poetry reading. She stands in the door, blinking.

She's *here*. There's a *now* again, and the scene is moving around her, and she only had time to wonder how she managed to enter that moment instead of watching it rush past, when she meets . . .

His eyes.

He stops, for the merest moment. Then there's a smile, surprised and pleased, and when he resumes reading, she is certain that he has seen her.

She takes an unsteady step toward one of the chairs and sits down and listens to the voice she still hears when she opens the poetry book. Some of the lines break her heart. She sits in perfect stillness, part of her still unable to believe where she is. It cannot be real. Her body is still being destroyed and made whole again inside the machine; nothing in her calculations ever predicted that her entire self, body and mind, would be allowed to travel back in time for good. But as the scientist in her keeps pondering hypotheses and teasing plausible leads apart from fancies, the rest of her takes in the moment she has miraculously managed to find, and she listens, and lets *now* stretch until forever.

She rises after the applause has died down. She stands at the back of the room, as a couple of people walk up to him to offer congratulations. He exchanges a few words with them, though he steals glances at her from time to time.

At last, he crosses the room. She feels the smile pull at her lips just as her heart starts breaking all over again. He greets her with a kiss on each cheek and a hand gently resting on her arm.

"I thought you wouldn't be able to make it!" he says.

"I made time," she replies.

He smiles. There's something in his eyes, awed and uncertain all at once. His hand hasn't left her arm.

"Thank you," he simply says. And then—"You look lovely tonight."

She wonders how different she seems to him. She's fifteen years older, much closer to his age now. She's thought a lot, seen a lot. Her throat swells, briefly. There could have been a future in another rivulet, for the woman she's now, for the man he still is. There are so many things she would like to tell him.

But she already knows she won't say them. If this had been an illusion, a figment of her dying mind, she might have indulged. She had thought it might be, until she felt the gentle, careful contact of his hand on her arm, so familiar after all these years, though she had long forgotten what it felt like. Never mind how she managed to access this moment—or rather, never mind that she already, heartbreakingly, understands that her body will claim her back from it like daylight after a dream—it is real, much too real to spoil with words neither of them would know how to handle once they were out in the open. This is what she wanted, this greeting, friends meeting again after a long time, far longer for her than it has been for him.

"I wanted to see you," she says instead, knowing that he will never suspect how earnestly she means it.

They walk out together. She glances at him once or twice and catches a furtive glance from him as she does so. They talk some more, none of it touching on anything she had wanted to say. It is all right. This is what she had wished for: their effortless conversations, the equally effortless silences between words. A few minutes—then they leave the campus, and he stops, right at the place where she usually turns right toward home, while he turns left.

She toys with the idea of offering to go to his hotel with him. She doesn't, in the end. That moment no longer belongs to her. She wraps her arms around him and hugs him more fiercely than she ever has.

"Good night," she whispers.

She turns around once, to watch him walk away. He doesn't look back.

And then he's gone.

Two days later, she—that younger she, the one who could not make it to the reading—will learn through the online poetry board she frequents on occasion that his heart failed, and he passed away in his hotel, hours after reading his final texts out loud. She will stare at the screen for over an hour. She will not mention it to anyone. Theirs was not an official sort of friendship, one of mutual invitations, parties, and holiday cards. She had never met his family. She will not go to the funeral, though that day, she will put on a flowery dress and walk on her own in the wild hills they liked to gaze at from the terrace of the café.

She will never delete her final text to him.

The time traveler exits the machine and turns off the power.

It is dark in the lab. It is dark, also, when she crosses the door of her home; her daughter is awake, nonetheless. Her face falls a little when she sees her mother shamble home, then lifts when the time traveler takes her in her arms and hugs her for long moments, smiling over her shoulder at her husband.

You don't yearn for what you already have. You bask in it, one moment after another, and there is no room to wish, to ponder *what ifs* until they make your heart hurt. That does not make the love less real.

"I'm home now, darling," she whispers. "I'm home."

Her daughter yawns. She carries her to her bedroom and watches her fall asleep, before sinking into her own bed and falling asleep in turn, holding her husband's hand.

Her life is filled with beauty, and fulfilment, and with wonder she is grateful for. She makes up her mind to stay home the next day. And maybe a few days after that, enjoying the quiet, the rumble of her daughter's hurried footsteps, the strange caress of the spring air, the hushed sensations of a body that is, against the odds, still very much alive.

But as she sinks into an undisturbed sleep, she dreams of a long-lost face, kind, sharp, smiling eyes peering at her through a curtain of water, and a hand outstretched, in greeting, in invitation.

She leans into the waterfall and closes her eyes against the rushing water. She kisses him there, and his hands come to rest on her back, and a moment that never happened engraves itself into the rock below, where reality dwells forever.

ABOUT THE AUTHOR

Cécile Cristofari lives in South France, where she teaches English literature and writes stories when her children are asleep. Her fiction has previously appeared in *Interzone, Daily Science Fiction, Reckoning,* and others. Her debut short story collection, *Elephants in Bloom,* was recently published by Newcon Press.

Binomial Nomenclature and the Mother of Happiness

ALEXANDRA MUNCK

1

When I first came to Alamogordo-20, the pool wasn't a popular spot. It sat in full blazing sun, not quite rectangular, concrete the color of plantar warts. People came to swim laps in the evening, but it wasn't right for socializing. Then Environmental Engineering adopted it. They installed a synthetic verge and shade towers that produced misted breezes. All of a sudden, you saw groups of people walking down Main Street in sandals with towels over their shoulders. I'm taking the time to explain this about the pool so you'll understand why Colleague A and I had the conversation we did.

We were relaxing after work, sitting with our feet in the deep end. Colleague A is an astrophysicist, a prominent name in her field, and I was enjoying being seen with her. People we knew drifted over, saying things like "Didn't Environmental do a great job?" or "The towers are so clever aren't they?"

It was after a number of these comments that Colleague A turned to me and said, "Imagine if they knew Astrophysics discovered that Earth has three moons."

Almost as soon as the words left her mouth, her eyes reacted to them. Colleague A has strangely expressive eyes. They remind me of the eyes in cel-animated family films, large and exaggerated by design, so that even preverbal children can follow exactly how the characters are feeling.

"Oh lord," she said, putting a hand on my forearm. "I wasn't supposed to say that. You can't tell anybody."

I wanted to ask her about the moons, but that would have been an even worse breach of protocol. Astrophysics is one of the most highly classified divisions in Alamogordo-20. Instead of giving in to my curiosity and pressuring her to compound her error, I decided, for politeness' sake, to downplay what had just happened.

"Slip of the tongue," I said. "Let's forget about it."

I expected her to be relieved, me letting her off the hook like that. Instead, she made frustrated eyes. You would think those eyes would put her at a disadvantage with people, giving things away, but they also have a certain power to make you feel however she wants you to feel. Right then, they were making me feel as though it was I who had broken the rules. I looked down at my feet in the water, noticing how the distortion of light disconnected them from my ankles. I wondered why everyone was at the pool. Not much had changed. The locker rooms were still in bad shape. The concrete was the same sulky yellow.

Colleague A, dissatisfied with me, leaned in closer.

"Sonder matter," she whispered. "Two unknown moons made entirely of sonder matter." She must have seen the astonishment on my face, because her lips formed a tiny twist of a smile. "Just so you aren't confused. Obviously, I wasn't talking about man-made satellites. Let's drop it now."

I don't think I said anything in response. It was too dangerous for me to know more. Astrophysics had invented an instrument that could directly detect sonder matter, a substance so strange and elusive, its very name sounded to me like a fairy tale? But I never asked for that information. I had no legitimate reason to be interested. I acted like I didn't care, and now Colleague A let me.

We're busy these days in Animal Behavioral Science, especially with Angela finally getting pregnant. I don't want you to think we aren't working as hard as the other divisions. You should know that I'm not a zoologist. I was recruited to Alamogordo-20 when Animal Behavior requested a dedicated hardware engineer. Animal Behavior isn't exactly a prestigious assignment; we're not at the forefront of the sorts of scientific breakthroughs that change the world. But new recruits in the big Engineering divisions like Autocraft, Weaponry, even Environmental, all they do all day is take orders that come down the military chain of command. In Animal Behavior, I'm my own boss.

Other engineers get nervous around me. "Pretty quiet over there, isn't it?" some of them say. They're embarrassed that they are doing more important work, classified work that they can't talk to me about. But these comments never bother me. "Oh yeah, real quiet," I say. "Except for the howler monkeys."

As I mentioned, Angela is pregnant. She told me one morning about a week ago when I was walking past on my way to work.

"Hello," she said. "Will you come over?"

I approached the fence.

"Yes, Angela?"

She doesn't usually call me over to talk, even though I walk by every morning. We chat when I'm fitting new devices, or adjusting her old ones, but that only happens every month or so.

"I have wonderful news," she said. "I am with child."

I remember smiling up at her large face. I may even have laughed. It was a very happy surprise, and a huge relief.

"Angela!" I said. "Congratulations. How do you feel?"

She waved her trunk, wiggling the tip through one of the honeycomb gaps in her fence.

"I feel like a Tandoori To Go."

"A what?" I asked.

"It's something from my screen. I don't select it, but it plays in the middle of my videos."

"You watch commercials?"

Now that she had given me this context, I recalled seeing that particular ad. The Tandoori To Go is the name of an electric tandoor oven, a sleek stainless-steel cylinder with a drawer on one side. In the ad, a hand appears and pops open the drawer. A family, hovering around, make exaggerated sad faces when they see that it is empty. Then the hand shows them how to add meat and rice and a spice mix. The next time the drawer pops open, steam rises, and dinner is revealed. The family cheers and claps.

"Your keepers know?"

"I told them first thing this morning. Now they are running needle tests."

Angela hates blood draws, but I could tell she was more than willing to submit to any procedure pertaining to being *with child.*

"You seem pleased with yourself," I said.

"Very pleased, yes."

The zoologists have been trying to get Angela pregnant for years. Every few months, they fertilize a few of her eggs and implant them, and every few months, nothing. Until now. I wonder if Angela understands what having a baby will really mean, eventually. For now, she's the center of attention. We even threw a party for her. I invited Colleague A.

"A baby shower for a talking elephant," she said. "How can I say no to that?"

I met her at the Observatory after work. It is built right into the western summit of the mountain, a rather fanciful setting, until you get inside, and then it looks like any other industrial lab building. Glass windows offer a view of military facilities down in the pale desert flats. Security left us alone after Colleague A vouched for me. She was finishing up for the day, perched on an ancient swivel chair beneath a dome of light and reflective metal. Astrophysics is finished with real human eyes, but they keep the optical telescope around because visible impressions of space are still in demand with the public. The sheer largeness of it made me feel respectful, as though I was looking at the mausoleum of a once mighty king.

Completely obsolete, needless to say. I think that's why, when Colleague A motioned me toward the seat with the optical interface, I sat down without worrying that I was breaking protocol. I scrolled through a slideshow of images captured by the telescope's cameras. Spiral galaxies and comets and the veiny Crab Nebula and two suns tugging at each other. Standard, useless pictures, artificially punched up with orange and yellow and magenta, probably already declassified and published.

The last image in the slideshow was not colorized. Furry objects appeared sunken, as though they were living deep inside of the flat picture: twin spheroids, just like the kind normal people imagine when they think of outer space. But not like. They seemed to sibilate. Two coronas of insectile static embraced them in riblike pulses, something like an electromagnetic field, maybe, but entirely the wrong shape. I felt Colleague A at my shoulder.

"What are they?" I asked, even though I already knew.

"Shit," she said. "That wasn't supposed to be in there. Look, forget you saw it."

"Are they the moons?"

I would have thought she'd be irritated with me for asking questions I wasn't allowed to ask, and which she would get into serious trouble for answering, but instead her eyes became fierce and gleaming with satisfaction.

"We named them yesterday. Palikos alpha and Palikos beta. Can you believe it was this old dinosaur that found them?"

I should have stopped her then. All I can say is that I did not. She patted the metallic hide of the optical telescope and began to explain the process that allowed it to produce images of sonder matter. A lot of hard work had gone into the project, apparently. The technology was classified supersecret and likely to stay that way for at least a generation.

When she finished, I said, "Apply for a formal collaboration with me."

I could see her real surprise. This wasn't what she'd been expecting at all. I'm still not sure how she wanted me to react to what she confided in me, only that she wanted some sort of reaction, and it wasn't this one. But how could she be surprised? Had she forgotten I was a scientist too, with ambitions beyond making wearable gadgets for zoo animals?

She asked me why.

"I want to try to adapt this imaging process into something smaller. Something portable."

"What use would that be?" she said. "Besides, Animal Behavioral Science? They'd think I was joking."

Her eyes were now telling me to feel like a child in an art museum. You can *look*, but don't *touch*.

"Disclose our personal relationship to your head of engineering. Tell him I'm bored with nothing to do over in Animal Behavior." This wasn't true, but it would sound believable. Any fellow engineer would sympathize. "Say I'm talented but frustrated. A successful collaboration, resulting in or even ruling out new applications of this technology, could be my ticket to bigger things."

We left for the party without settling anything, and I thought nothing would come of it. But an approval arrived yesterday along with a sinkhole of heavily redacted data and an acerbic personal note from one of the military higher-ups in Astrophysics.

Putter all you want, it says. The *you poor bastard* is implied.

Even taking into account what happened at Angela's shower, I think Colleague A only submitted the request because she assumed it would be denied. I wonder if I've made her angry. I find Colleague A easier to read than most people, but she can still be confusing at times. Maybe I have pushed too far. Maybe this has been inappropriate in the extreme. On the other hand, the portable sonder matter viewer is likely to be a total dead end. Probably I will turn it on, look through it, and see nothing.

I have already begun the work.

2

Yesterday I saw sonder matter through my portable imager for the first time. Considering the information and materials I've been working with, I'm pleased to be getting any results, even if they puzzle me.

I began by looking for the Palikos moons. I have waited so long to see them again. I don't know when they are in the sky, so perhaps I made my attempt at the wrong time, or my equipment is too weak to pick them up. The goggles are heavy. They cling to my face like something alive, dragging my head earthward. But it turns out there is sonder matter anywhere you look.

If you've ever taken a computer history course, you may have seen some of the earliest achievements in CGI: ovals and squares floating around in gray space. That is what flakes of sonder matter put me in mind of. They are perfectly textureless, and they pass through solid objects. I watched them drift through the meat of my outstretched hand. Into the palm and out again through the back, uncaught. They appear to be two-dimensional. Without any depth to set them off, they look pasted onto their background. They don't reflect light or cast shadows. When they rotate, they seem to wink in and out of existence. I followed them until my neck ached, first one, then another, like a child in a snow flurry. At some point, I heard a heavy step approaching and almost simultaneously bumped into a fence.

"Good evening, Angela," I said. "Why are you out here so late?"

Angela is about five months along now. The excitement of early pregnancy has worn off, and she tires easily, often going to sleep with the sun.

She didn't acknowledge me right away, staring at something in the distance. After a moment, she shifted her weight and flapped her ears. "It's nothing, only some of my keepers."

"What do you mean?"

"They're discussing me." She curled her trunk to touch her forehead. "I'm very important around here, you know."

An eddy of sonder matter flakes swirled out of her upraised trunk.

My aunt used to have a lot of Lichtenstein pop art prints around her apartment. We ate dinner and tidied up and played chess and went to sleep before an audience of crying Lichtenstein women. The small, square flakes that came from Angela's trunk reminded me of those pictures. The women's tears, flat and luminous, never felt as though they had a physical relationship with the eyes that were shedding them. Small alien births. And I was struck by the sudden extrusion for another reason: most of the sonder matter I had observed to this point moved east to west through my field of vision, as if borne on a current, and had no visible source.

"You are," I told Angela. "Very, very important."

I peered through the fence. With the goggles on, anything that is not sonder matter has a fuzzy, low-definition appearance. Lights were blazing inside Angela's indoor habitat, and the large steel service door was rolled up. I could see two figures. I heard a snatch of their conversation and recognized the voice of Angela's head keeper, Colleague B. He was gesturing at a woman. The woman was shaking her head. I didn't recognize her, and for a few moments I was completely absorbed in trying to figure out who she was.

I didn't mean to eavesdrop. I'm not sure why I stayed, when under normal circumstances I would have tried to avoid hearing anything private. Perhaps it was because I couldn't immediately identify the woman with Colleague B. Something about the goggles contributed, too. They make me feel I'm not part of the world anymore, as though I am standing at a remove. Now that I think about it, the way the flakes are in such sharp focus compared to everything else in the visual field is probably the root cause of this feeling. In fact, the goggles encourage the user to identify with the sonder matter. I should try to fix that.

Whatever the reason, instead of backing off, I pressed in closer. I finally recognized the woman as one of our divisional heads.

"I do think it's for the best," she was saying.

Colleague B made a noise that sounded like a laugh but was really something else altogether. I didn't quite catch what he said in response. I heard the phrases "maternal bonding" and "natural pregnancy." I should mention at this point that I have worked with Colleague B for three years, closely at times. I recognized strain in his voice, even though he was trying to keep the discussion friendly.

They drifted to the edge of the pooling light. The woman was saying, "I have the authority to make this decision, and I believe I am making the safest choice, the most fruitful choice for our future."

"So it's final?"

"As soon as the mother can be prepared," she said. "An explanation is not beyond her."

"No," he said. "An explanation is not."

"I'm sure she'll want what's best for her baby, once she has come to understand the situation."

Colleague B nodded.

"Then you agree?"

Colleague B's face was at low resolution in the goggles, but I filled in the details of his smile that I could not see. I knew he was smiling. He was probably humming under his breath.

"Yes," he said. "Yes, I guess you're right after all."

At the very moment Colleague B said this, about the woman being right after all, a torrent of flakes erupted from his shoulders. Thin, filament-like strokes burst around him, dying and flashing back into focus at a furious rate. For a heartbeat they unfurled, in a seemingly organized way, as wings do. This illusion of coordination was broken a second later, and they dissipated into the night. Most of them floated westward through the cement wall of Angela's habitat, streaking the air like a miniature lightning storm. The whole time, Colleague B was smiling his easygoing, self-effacing smile. Underneath, I was nearly sure that he was seething. It's not that there's anything special about Colleague B, but I've worked closely with him on Angela's equipment, and people who work together end up noticing these things. It's a perfectly natural consequence of social intercourse. For instance, he hums when he's concentrating. I don't think he knows that he does it.

I instantly hypothesized that the unexpected sonder matter explosion was representative of Colleague B's true feelings. Had his emotional response actually produced the flakes? I am sure it was no coincidence, although I will need to conduct more observational studies to verify. The difference in shape between the thin, branching spikes and Angela's teardrops is suggestive.

At some point, Colleague B noticed me watching.

"Who's there?" he called.

I should have said something. Normally, of course, I would have. Perhaps I was overwhelmed with new data, but just at that moment saying hello seemed difficult. I shrank away from the fence as he approached. The goggles seemed to weigh on me again, pulling my head down. I saw a liquid line spurt from my stomach, a Lichtenstein tear, and for a strange moment I thought I had been shot.

"Oh, it's only you. I suppose you heard all that."

When I finally raised my chin, he was close, just on the other side of the fence. Angela had gone off somewhere to sleep.

"No." I shook my head, which made the sonder matter blink and swarm. Was it all flakes of leftover emotion? Spectral recordings of other conversations, other arguments, suppressed joys and frustrations mingling and drifting away together? "Not really."

I don't usually lie, but I didn't want to embarrass him. He stared at me for a second or two, studying the goggles. Then he looked up at the sky, ruffling his hair with one hand and blowing out a sigh.

"Well, it's not some big secret. You probably know the pregnancy isn't going as well as it could be. The fetus is small. Within safety limits, but small. The Division wants to transfer it to the artificial uterus as soon as possible to guarantee a positive outcome. Well, I say nothing is guaranteed. I am worried Angela won't bond with it if we take it out of her. She already seems to consider it an accessory, a proof of her own consequence."

He must have gotten tired of standing there when I didn't say anything. I was too busy watching him carefully. Little Cheerio-shaped things were coming out of his ears, waning into nothingness, waxing again like hollow moons.

"I'm sure it doesn't interest you much. It's not your side of things."

It finally occurred to me what to say. "I can get the artificial uterus ready in case it's needed. I'll do it right away. I'll make sure it's all right."

He gave me a crooked smile. The Cheerio flakes stopped, and no more flakes fell.

"Oh, certainly," he said. "I had no doubt. As I said, it's not that part of it that has me worried."

I nodded and felt a strong urge to retreat before he asked me about the goggles. I would have had to disappoint him by telling him that they're classified. Anyway, now that I have got them working, I have a lot of fine-tuning to do. I want to improve the visual experience for the user. And there are questions that need answering. How many observably distinct shapes of sonder matter are there? Is shape a superficial characteristic or does it point to qualitative differences? Can a taxonomy be created? There is a considerable amount of work ahead of me.

Also, I have an artificial uterus to overhaul.

3

Colleague A keeps trying to get me out to the pool again. I wish I could say yes. I know she thinks that my lack of interest in socializing has something to do with what happened at Angela's baby shower. But that was months ago. The truth is, I'm fully engrossed in the goggles. Everywhere I go, flakes fall in a sideways rain. Their very flatness and smoothness have the power to disorient me. Sometimes my perception switches, and instead of blinking, rotating flakes, I see the world tearing itself apart. Depth isn't real, the scenery around me is only a thin layer of paint hiding pale cold nothingness. It shouldn't be addictive.

My taxonomy is still in its earliest stages.

Maestitia, called sorrow, is oval. I have produced it artificially by watching sad films.

Laetitia, joy, small and square. Resembles glitter or confetti. I observe it when groups of people laugh together. Dogs emit great clouds of it.

Ira, anger. This is the one that looks like lightning, like children scribbling in the air with sparklers on the Fourth of July. I most recently observed it when I was passing the gorilla habitat during a therapeutic provocation session, tornadoing out of the silverback's chest.

Metus, fear. The Cheerio-shaped flakes. Can be produced in stacks that resemble those fossilized crinoids you sometimes find in the pale-yellow escarpments around here.

These are only rough categories. There is great variation of shape within each group, so that they are difficult to differentiate when you see them in real time. I have tried to watch carefully. The flakes show only slivers of themselves, rotating in and out of view, flashing like slick minnows, dripping out of my own body, blending together as they float off. But I am not discouraged. Just recently, I added continuous video capture to the goggles, which has been a big help. I anticipate, in the future, refining my taxonomy. Joy, sorrow, anger, fear: these are not species of emotion, but kingdoms. I will use binomial nomenclature. Maybe this sounds far-fetched, but I do have some evidence to support my hypothesis. One example is the *metus* shed by Colleague B the night I made my first observations. Could he really have been feeling true fear, looking at me? The same sort of fear you'd feel watching a horror film? Isn't it more likely he was feeling something a bit different? There are a lot of reasons someone might feel nervous to talk to another person, and not all of them are negative. So you see, I am not discouraged at all.

Increasingly, I am convinced that the flatness of the flakes disguises even greater variety. Emotions can't really exist in only two dimensions. Do they feel like they do? If I continue to improve my goggles, maybe I will come to see a hidden depth. Often they drag my head down, and I watch what is sprouting from my belly.

What is love, I wonder? Is it an undiscovered species of happiness? Of sorrow?

Does it exist, measurably speaking?

Don't judge me for this preoccupation. If you were in my position, you would want to know what love looks like, too.

4

"Is it possible for you to predict the future?"

I was running a routine check on Angela's voice box. I had been asking her to repeat strings of words with specific phonemes, but this was her own question.

"What do you mean?" I said. "How could I do that?"

"Maybe you could build a machine to do it."

Mah-*sheen*. I heard a slight catch in her pronunciation, an upward modulation, and paused my checklist.

"Say 'machine' again."

I was occupied for a few minutes with this. Afterward I asked her, "What is it you want to know about the future?"

"Oh, nothing. But the prophecies of the witches caused so much trouble for Macbeth, I was thinking that if they could be produced by machine it might make them more precise, and safer."

Mah-*sheen*. There it was again, her voice blipping up into a higher register.

I know Colleague B has been doing enrichment activities with Angela to take her mind off her son, currently gestating in the large artificial uterus in the Central Veterinary Building. He told me about it the day before yesterday. Part of his work is conducting research on Angela's creative capabilities, and her understanding of literature and fine art. Based on initial tests, he is optimistic that his line of inquiry will produce noteworthy results.

"So you've been reading Shakespeare?"

"My keeper says that Mr. William Shakespeare is the greatest writer the world has yet produced."

"Does he say that?"

"Oh, yes. He says that Mr. Shakespeare knows everything about life, and about love, and about hate, and about vengeance."

I have to admit my mind wasn't on our conversation. In addition to recalibrating Angela's voice box, I was daydreaming about a new plan to improve my goggles. I was wearing them at the time. I wear them often, now that they don't interfere with my ability to do my other work. Angela told me they make my eyes look funny, like an insect's eyes. She went on, summarizing the plot of Macbeth, but I can't be sure that was all she said. I wasn't paying close attention.

I noticed suddenly that oversized flakes of *metus* were falling from her belly. There were so many of them, together they almost took on another dimension. I staggered back in alarm. My eyes tried to fight the image, to make sense of it: for a moment, it looked as though someone was squatting inside her stomach cavity with a large drill, boring a hole. The dense column poured out of her straight into the ground, only a few flakes getting caught in the westward current. The picture was so disturbing, I produced my own *metus* that obscured my vision.

"It's going to be okay," Angela said. "I'm going to take care of it soon."

I think that's what she said, but I can't be sure. Like I told you, I don't know where the conversation had gone, and it was all over soon after.

The flow of *metus* slowed to a trickle and then stopped. I finished my work and left.

But there is something about the incident that worries me. I am trying to resolve my discomfort by focusing on ideas for a new imager. Even though the apparent dimensionality of the *metus* column was an optical illusion, it's inspiring me to push forward. I have to learn more. I'm afraid of what might happen if I can't understand.

I'm going to take care of it soon. The dark drill bit screwed into the ground. *I'm going to take care of it soon,* she said, with enough power to penetrate solid earth. That type of fear will have consequences.

5

I admit to being careful, especially with how fast things are happening now. If you change the order of operations in an equation, you can complete each step correctly and still end up with the wrong result. I don't want to write true things that accidentally convey an incorrect meaning. The overall outcome of this situation, correctly interpreted, is how pleased I am to have solved my depth problem. I have discovered several new subspecies of sonder matter, and my taxonomy can finally move forward. I want that point firmly underlined, especially since, as I say, things are happening fast.

I had just finished a major upgrade to my goggles when Colleague A called. She's been insistent recently on setting up a lunch date for us, but I've been so busy I really haven't been able to spare the time. Today I said yes because I wanted to take the new goggles on a test run. I didn't put them on at first and instead wore the old model. As I walked down Main Street from my apartment, I savored my last sight of two-dimensional sonder matter. We had a beautiful day here, not too hot, and *laetitia* clouded the passersby: soldiers, scientists, support staff out enjoying the sunshine. I remember thinking that I would slip on the new goggles when I sat down at the café. I would then be able to see the splits in *laetitia*, the cracks between every shade of happiness.

I got a table near the window. While I was sitting there, waiting for Colleague A, a woman on the sidewalk stopped and stared at the glass. She was shedding tiny, O-shaped *metus*. Then she bared her teeth like the rhesus monkeys in Animal Behavior when they are signaling submissiveness. She ran her tongue over her teeth and began to fix her hair.

The bell on the door tinkled. A wreath of *laetitia* hung around Colleague A as she waved at me and made her way over to the table. She was generating it out of her shoulders. The small flakes rose like black motes swimming upward off a hot desert highway, and I wondered if my shoulders looked the same, as though putting your hands on them would result in burns.

"Hey stranger," she said. "Feels like it's been such a long time, doesn't it?"

"Not even half an elephant pregnancy."

We fell into talking about Angela. For an astrophysicist, she seemed to know a lot about how Angela was doing. I even remarked, just in a casual way, that she seemed to know an awful lot about Angela and all of her pregnancy woes.

"Well, Colleague B and I have been talking."

She used his real name, of course. She used his first name, in fact, which I could not help but remember I had not used when I introduced the two of them at Angela's baby shower.

"It's nothing, really, not anything I would have bothered mentioning if you hadn't brought it up. Mostly we talk about you. Well, to tell you the truth, we're worried about you."

I inspected her for worry. Her eyes communicated concern, but *laetitia* was still pouring out of her shoulders. I wondered if my new goggles would reveal this to be a false classification. Maybe her apparent hypocrisy wasn't what it looked like. In the meantime, I had to find a way to continue the conversation. I was about to reply, "Why do you say that?" when I noticed Colleague B through the plate glass window. He was on the sidewalk, looking up at the awning of the café. Then he took one big step forward, and I heard the tinkle of the door.

"Did you invite him?" I asked.

Colleague A laughed. "You're so paranoid." But she didn't turn around to look.

Colleague B wandered through the café as though unconscious of us and verbally expressed surprise when he bumped into our table with his hip. But I saw no emotional reaction from him at all. I don't think he was surprised. I think he was expecting to find us. We exchanged greetings.

"How've you been?" he asked. He peered hard at me, trying to see behind my goggles.

I said something about making progress in my research.

"Angela has been asking about you. She seems to have developed a liking for you. She's become more and more withdrawn lately."

He was fingering the edge of a sugar packet. Unlike Colleague A, who was still clouded with some species of happiness, he did have *metus* coming out of his ears. Little worried flakes, like the woman I had seen inspecting her appearance in the window but deformed slightly. As they rotated, I got a sense of their odd shape. Interesting, but nothing compared to what I was about to see. I realized that while I was parsing this visual, he had been waiting for me to speak.

"I don't know exactly what you're working on," he said, tapping the sugar packet, "but do you think anything in your research could help?"

I reminded him that my research was classified. I immediately turned to look at Colleague A, watching me closely from across the table.

"Of course I'd like to be of help," I said. "But it's against the rules. I don't know where you got the idea that what I'm working on has any potential application for Angela."

Colleague A and Colleague B exchanged glances.

Technically, I have been working with Astrophysics this whole time. I have been sending my reports to Astrophysics' head of engineering, as directed by the Collaboration Order. But he isn't free to divulge details about my work to Colleague A, who, after all, is not an engineer. I've already been in violation of Alamagordo-20's strict secrecy protocols, as I have admitted to you, and although it was through no fault of my own, I found the experience uncomfortable and too distressing to repeat. But it is true (and I've learned this only gradually) that a predictable percentage of the people here, in the course of things, do become somewhat lax.

It dawned on me that they knew.

Colleague A smiled at me, gently. Her shoulder was touching Colleague B's shoulder.

"I'll be honest with you," she said. "We—"

"Just a second."

I'm not sure why I decided on that particular moment. Maybe I just needed a pause in conversation while I processed this new information. I reached into my bag for the updated goggles and put them on. They are somewhat bulkier than all of their predecessors while also being lighter, much lighter.

Colleague B was watching me with an unreadable expression. But what I saw coming off him was wonderfully specific: intricately ridged, three-dimensional toroids. *Metus,* I was sure of it. The flakes, although I can't call them flakes anymore, not now that I know what they really look like. The sonder matter bodies, I will say. The sonder matter bodies were buckled and warped, like twisted old automobile tires. Despite their third dimension, they retained that essential alienness, refusing to relate to their background. They hovered around us like glowing UFOs. There you have it, I told myself, the goggles work. *This* is a moment of real scientific triumph. And I told myself, just think. Soon you will look back at *this* moment, and you will identify that exact species of *metus*, and you will know for sure what he is feeling, in his heart of hearts, in his most vulnerable and reactive flesh, just exactly . . . now.

I must have let my excitement distract me because I forgot to invite Colleague A to continue. Finally, Colleague B said: "Colleague A has filled me in on what you're doing. I know it's against regulations, but my main concern is Angela, and I have to pursue every possible solution. If I could wear those things when I work with her, then at least I would have some concrete data about her emotional state. I would be able to measure her reactions to different stimuli."

Here's what I mean about things happening fast: by the time Colleague B was sitting down at our table in the café, Angela had already attacked the artificial uterus. At some point after he left her habitat, and it must have been quite soon after, she asked one of the assistant keepers to escort her to the Central Veterinary Building "to see her baby." The uterus is visible through a ground floor window. According to witnesses, she spent several minutes watching it until, with no warning, she put her ears back and charged. It ended this way: with one of her front legs through the window, lacerated all over by shards of glass, and one of her tusks scraping the wall, thrusting and gouging but unable to reach the uterus.

"The problem is," Colleague B was saying, "we don't know how she really feels toward her baby. She's been reticent and moody, but I can't tell if that's due to her physical recovery from the transplantation procedure. Maybe something entirely different is bothering her. She won't talk to me about it. I'm concerned that the mother-offspring bond has been damaged. My highest priority right now is fostering that bond. We need Angela to be a good mother."

Colleague A leaned forward and squeezed my arm. "Come on, we could really help him." She added my first name to the end of her sentence for emphasis. "If you're worried about the classification protocols, we can apply for another collaboration and make it official."

Little wormlike things began to crawl out of her hair. A second species of *metus*, hollow, like macaroni noodles. They dropped, writhing, through the table. I saw by this that Colleague A was more worried about gaining insight into my discoveries around sonder matter than she was about me, as she had claimed.

I said, "I'd like to help Angela, but unfortunately, the details of my research are classified."

Colleague A looked at me hard, and this time her eyes matched her emotion. *Metus* was soon eclipsed by *ira*. *Ira,* unmistakably. The thin bodies precipitated out of her head like a rapidly growing thornbush, like water vapor freezing into ice. This was really quite beautiful to see. *Ira* laced out of her head, as I said, but also out of her arms, and her broad chest, and I believe, if I had looked under the table, I would have seen it sprouting in all the cracks between her toes.

"Why do you have to be so selfish?" she snapped. She shoved her chair back and stalked away in the direction of the restroom, dropping sharp cotton candy clouds of anger.

"She doesn't really care about Angela at all," I told Colleague B. "She just wants to get her hands on my research."

He was by this time shedding some of the same feather-like *ira* I had first seen as unfurling wings.

"I'm not speculating," I told him, and I indicated my goggles. I smiled at him and waited for him to return it. I waited.

"I know," he said. "But you can understand how she's feeling, can't you? She led the team that made the breakthrough in the first place with that old optical telescope. A major discovery that was immediately taken out of her hands by National Security, assorted generals, and a bunch of people so high up we don't even know who they are. Now here you are, one-upping her, wearing her hard work on your face and claiming you own it. After she was generous enough to share with you in the first place."

His *ira* flared, and I realized it was for me.

I couldn't see for a few moments afterward, because a particularly thick emission of sonder matter bodies appeared in front of me just then. When they dissipated, I saw Colleague B staring at me, arms crossed.

"Is this about our relationship?"

I did not answer. I had to make sure the goggles were recording, so I did not answer.

"We got together pretty fast," he said, "and she thinks it might have made you uncomfortable. That night at the baby shower. She thinks it's why you keep refusing to see her."

"I don't refuse to see her," I said. "I'm just really busy."

He sighed and uncrossed his arms. "Okay."

Do you remember what I said before about the order of operations and getting correct results? Please apply that now because I fear this might be easy to misunderstand: the way Colleague B was looking at me then, he looked sad. It was a genuine expression. His eyes are always genuine, unlike the way Colleague A uses hers at times. He was feeling sad for me. But what I saw coming from him, falling from the corners of his mouth, was small and cuboid. Clearly a species of *laetitia*. I used the eye-twitch controls in the new goggles, zooming in, isolating, imaging, imaging, imaging. It is the most important thing I have discovered thus far: that pity is a species of happiness. That's only a preliminary conclusion, obviously, but you have to admit, it is very exciting. I feel that even more fascinating insights wait just over the horizon. When my research is finally declassified and published, psychologists will be rushing to congratulate me. *This* moment is only and forever a *major breakthrough* in scientific history. And that is why tonight I will be celebrating with a few drinks in private.

6

The conversation in the café, because it represents a major career success, is still at the top of my mind. But in Animal Behavior the talk is all about Angela's attempted attack on her unborn fetus. I overheard several comments just today, as I was out working on my beta taxonomy.

"You forget sometimes, with the genetic mods and the voice boxes, but they really are wild animals we're working with."

"Because they speak so well, you expect them to reason. You start to think that they see the world the same way you do and are not absolutely ruled by instinct."

"They demand that we respect their wildness. I think Angela's wildness has been disrespected, just because she is the most intelligent."

I did not offer any opinions of my own. I don't think that what she did has anything to do with her so-called wildness, however. Natural selection is brutally logical; animal instinct is not typically expressed in the killing of one's young. Certainly not when one is well-fed, housed, exercised, and cared for by affectionate keepers. This behavior of hers seems quite human to me. Modern humans, it seems to me, live in a reality that is based upon rational extrapolation from all of our indirect sources of information. We build teetering towers of evermore abstract thought pasted together by theory and colored by our sonder matter extrusions. Emotions plus rational thought equal reason, and the ability to reason equals the ability to go mad. To fear things that are not threats. We who go beyond natural selection, it seems to me, are out here looking for trouble.

I have a confession of sorts. Sometimes when I am walking by Colleague B's office, I see his feelings drift through the wall. His office is on the second floor of Angela's building, above her indoor habitat. There are two windows: a big sheet glass one inside that allows him to look down on Angela, and a small, clouded one on the exterior wall with a potted cactus on the sill. I'm almost sure it's dead. Some days it looks as though it has perked up, and other times I'm sure that it has entered an advanced state of decay. Difficult to tell from the ground. I have never been inside his office, only seen it through its two windows.

I walk by, and if there is a light on in the cactus window, I stop. I am usually already wearing my goggles, feeling the weight of them in the base of my skull as I stand in the shadow of the building and crane my neck and watch. I'm aware that this is embarrassing, and that I should be embarrassed. Still, I can't seem to stop myself. I feel as though I don't have any control when it comes to this particular habit. I usually manage to convince myself it's not so wrong, because all I can see are his feelings. I don't know what causes them. Some nights I play a guessing game about them. The angry sonder matter bodies are caused by work, the stress of Angela's pregnancy, and he is humming softly under his breath. Sorrow, in that particular presentation, means he is experiencing homesickness. I imagine him looking at pictures on his computer, clicking through a mother, a father, siblings, people that I don't know for sure exist. Other nights I don't guess. I don't want to know.

7

Angela was waiting for me by the fence tonight. Her front legs and parts of her trunk were bandaged in splatches of bright blue foam. The gate was closed, restricting her habitat temporarily to a small portion of the yard and her indoor room.

"Bug Eyes," she said. "Did you hear about my accident?"

"Was it an accident?" I said.

Her injured trunk traveled through the air, curling and uncurling. "That's what everyone is calling it. But listen. My keeper has said he wants me to write a story about it. He said it will help us both to understand why it happened."

"Did you write one?" I asked.

Pride welled up out of her forehead as she flapped her ears to imitate a human nod.

"Want to hear it, Bug Eyes? It's very short."

"Okay," I said.

She began to recite.

ANGELA'S VERY SHORT STORY

> Tandoori To Go was very nice. Her son, named Happiness, was not. But Tandoori To Go dealt with him very easily. She told him that if he misbehaved, he would find himself back inside her belly being burned up. From then on, Happiness says, it has been narrow escape after narrow escape.

"It's a good story, Angela," I said. "I've been trying my hand a little at writing, recently, but it's not my area of expertise. Still, I can say I find your story interesting."

"Thank you. I'm not sure what my keeper will think of it."

"Can I ask you a question?" I came up close to the fence, hooking my fingertips through the honeycomb. "Is Tandoori To Go lonely without Happiness?"

Angela shifted her weight. The *maestitia* she was shedding looked like smooth stones sinking to the bottom of a still pond.

"Yes, but it is not her choice to burn him up. It's the basic nature of Happiness that causes the problem." I looked up into her large, impassive face. "You're the one who seems lonely, Bug Eyes. Lonelier and lonelier since you put your bug eyes on. That's why I have been trying to make friends with you. Did you notice? Did it help?"

Happy pity replaced the *maestitia.* Pity from an elephant. It is one of those colorful anecdotes that can sometimes make science writing popular with the general public. Certainly another favorable outcome to add to the list of my recent favorable outcomes.

"Yes," I said, finally. "It was a big help. It really was." Her pity tangled with my own sonder bodies, and they drifted away together, rotating, separating, getting caught on the ghosts of other stray emotions. "What did you mean before when you said the basic nature of Happiness causes the problem? What is your son's basic nature?"

Angela stepped back and shifted her weight, an elephant wince. "He was taken from my womb."

Horror was screwing out of her stomach, trunk, knee joints, ears.

"So?" I tilted my head, watching her *metus*, imaging, imaging.

"He has a secret power," she said. "He can kill with impunity."

I stared at her. The *metus* intensified, her whole body quivering as she passed it.

"I don't understand," I said.

"Like Macduff," she whispered.

I lowered my chin to hide my smile from her. She could not see the burst of small, amused cubes. I swallowed and looked up again. "Angela," I said, "I think you have misunderstood Shakespeare."

"Did I?"

She shook her head, *metus* calming down.

"Don't worry," I said. "It happens to all of us. The truth is, just because someone is born by Caesarian section, or gestates in an artificial uterus, that doesn't mean that they are fated to kill anybody."

"Really?" Angela brightened considerably with this new information.

"Even though Shakespeare understood human nature deeply, and maybe knew something about elephant nature too, that's one of those things in the play that isn't true in real life. Like how nobody can predict the future."

Angela stamped her foot. "Is that right, Bug Eyes?"

"I swear it. You can ask your keeper, and he will tell you the same thing."

Angela stilled. Her trunk swayed low, brushing the ground, and a new species of *maestitia* dropped from her belly in long bowl-shaped hollows.

"Then I shouldn't have tried to kill him. Maybe I have turned into Lady Macbeth, now. There is blood on me that will not come off. That is her metaphor. Do you understand metaphors? I understand that one. My keeper explained it. The blood that will not come off. That's one of the things from the play that is true in real life. I see it on my tusks. They hosed me down, and it will not come off."

I looked closely. There were some stains on her tusks, dark brown. The blood was her own, of course. She had bled from the glass and made it worse by gashing her foot while thrusting around, head stuck in the broken window.

"That's because plain water can't get blood stains out of anything as porous as ivory," I said. "But have you heard of chlorine?"

I never rode on an elephant before. It is like rolling on a muscular sea. She knelt down with exceptional gentleness to guide me onto her back. I had not imagined that her trunk was so strong. Soon we were moving with irresistible, overwhelming force down Main Street, past the darkened café where I had seen something between Colleagues A and B. It wasn't love, was it? No, I don't think so. Past my apartment, which at the moment contains nothing that produces sonder matter bodies and cannot feel abandoned without me or miss the sound of my deep breathing on the right side of the bed. We have left behind some evidence of our passing. The honeycomb fence is twisted and broken now.

The pool has been improved in many ways, but it will never be good for stargazing. Mountain ridges rise steeply on either side, making the sky look half as wide and twice as deep. Angela stepped carefully into the shallow end. I went to the supply shed and retrieved the concentrated chlorine bleach that is normally added sparingly to the water. With the aid of towels and some rubber gloves, I polished her tusks until they were so white they seemed to glow in the dark, as though all of the excited energy within her was finally relaxing, surrendering photons like white handkerchiefs at the end of a war. We are sitting under one of the artificial shade towers, even though it is only just beginning to be dawn. We are watching the east, where there is a pinkness in the sky. Our eyes can sense what is happening on the other side of the ridge, even though we can't yet see the sun. The stars above the rocks are still visible, packed in like the points at the ends of line segments, specimens of *ira* pointed straight at us, of all people, heading toward us out of that fathomless afar. And I have finally found the moons. They've just come up over the mountain, two perfect orbs proceeding together in a parallel path across the sky. They rise fast, which gives the visual impression that they are lighter than the sun. With my newest pair of goggles, I can magnify them in my vision many times. And here is something interesting: they are swarming. The impression I get when I look at them is of ants on a cracked melon. Something is happening up there that was not captured by the still images from the optical telescope. The military obviously knows about it. No wonder Colleague A has been cut off from her own project. No wonder she is so desperate for my goggles. I can well believe this may be the most important scientific research in human history, much more important than my silly little taxonomy. If contact can be made, what might that open up? Such a delicate thing. It could go one way or the other. Maybe I have been selfish, after all.

As the moons race overhead, and with the edge of the lumbering sun finally showing itself, I've been daydreaming about reciprocity. Our worldly feelings, even those that go straight down through the Earth, must pass out of our atmosphere eventually and into space, just like radiation. From every direction, too, for all they seem to flow east to west around here. I am reminded of plasma flowing on the sun's surface. I imagine aliens with physical bodies made up entirely of sonder matter, each a little engine of fusion, radiating light simply by walking around and thinking and feeling. Them feeding us, us feeding them. Reciprocity. And I slide into a memory of Angela's baby shower, which was held in her indoor habitat. There was a folding table with a sheet cake from the café, and colored paper lanterns were strung on the staircase up to Colleague B's office. Angela was very hemmed in, but she was pleased with everything. She couldn't stop talking. I introduced Colleague A to her and went to get a slice of cake and a cup of fruit punch. The excitement of seeing those first images of the moons still hadn't left me. I remember my hand was shaking as I poured the punch. My entire being felt suddenly retracted, like the pupil of an eye when a bright light shines upon it, focused on one thing: those moons. Almost before I realized it, Colleague A and Colleague B had met each other and fallen deep into conversation. Seeing them talking like that gave me an unpleasant shock. Still, I couldn't stop thinking about sonder matter. It flowed through my mind as I watched. I followed them up the stairs and stood on the catwalk in front of Colleague B's office and looked in at what they were doing through that big window until they finally noticed me.

They were disturbed, I think. I only wanted to find out what was going on between them. The conversation that followed was uncomfortable. All the time, I was distracted. I couldn't stop thinking about those moons. Give me sonder matter, I said. You owe me. Break someone's heart, you owe them. Anyway, I don't know why I'm getting these old memories excited again. I don't even know the shape of heartbreak, I have been so busy. The collaboration came through and then my plate was full. They think I'm still spying on them, somehow, from behind my goggles, but I have given them their privacy. I only watch the outside of his office sometimes. Just on my way home. Just for a few minutes.

The sun is finally really gaining. We step out of the shade into clean light. I look over Angela's back and see a storm of sonder matter moving toward us against the usual flow. I can't make out any individual species yet. It's a dense soup. But we are gleaming for now, faultless and hard, until clouds blot out the sun.

ABOUT THE AUTHOR

Alexandra Munck is a writer in Chicagoland. Her fiction has appeared in *F&SF*, *Strange Horizons*, *Kenyon Review Online*, *Boulevard*, *The Cincinnati Review*, and is forthcoming in *Kaleidotrope*. She is currently at work on a children's novel.

Stars Don't Dream

CHI HUI, TRANSLATED BY JOHN CHU

1. The Shepherd

April, Mawlamyine.

The Shepherd leads her flock through a city half overgrown with weeds.

Weeds overwhelm the railway bridge, covering its deck. The pink wood sorrel has taken root in the road's cracked flower beds, depending on the lay of the terrain to fend off the twin assaults of dog's-tail grass and chicken feet grass. Hop vine holds the territory that crossties and crushed stone used to cover. The vine has spread its palm-shaped leaves recklessly around the barren clay. Boston ivy crosses the railings, winding like a wire. It climbs to the top of a utility pole, only to drop like a waterfall, weaving a green curtain at the end of the bridge.

A tunnel runs through the lower section of railway bridge. Its pavement is already covered by moss. Fat-hen pushes out relentlessly from the cracked cement. Bit by bit, they retake the battlefield for Nature from the creations of humanity.

The Shepherd leads her flock through the tunnel, up a gentle slope, to a wide plain. From there, she can see the nine, sky-scraping dream towers of the high-tech development zone as well as the semitransparent network of transport tracks interwoven among them. The tracks follow a silvery-white frame that extends from the ground up. They then spiral upwards wrapping themselves around each dream tower.

Express delivery drones flit around the towers like a swarm of bees. All of the bustle is concentrated in one place. In the distance is a long-abandoned city, and a park converted into grazing land.

The Shepherd finds a bench. Relaxed and at ease, she sits down.

She takes a count of her "flock": ten or so Iron Mans, thirty-something Ultramans, and four Gundam. They are assistive armored exoskeletons with customized exteriors, each one holding a living human body. A silver life-support web is spread throughout the armor. Slender electrodes stimulate and guide every muscle with exacting precision, letting the bodies get some exercise. They run, jump, stretch, and climb. Everything is precisely controlled to stay within the parameters for good health. When the sunlight isn't as intense, the armor becomes translucent, allowing the body inside to replenish vitamin D.

In the meantime, the consciousness each body sustains is immersed in the depths of a virtual world. Perhaps they are traveling among the stars, galloping across a battlefield, or spending an afternoon together with a lover. Holographic helmets give them a complete experience from sight to taste. It takes them through the stars, up into the sky, down into the abyss.

The Shepherd has visited one of the metaverse's enchanted worlds before. There, each step you take makes unusually substantial ripples in the air. The wind below your feet solidifies into glass. You can tread on the birdlike singing of flutes to enter the vault of heaven, where the aurora flows.

The illusions are boundless, but you'll have to leave your body in this world. Like an all-too-willing puppet, a joyful, flesh and blood, clockwork doll, you offer your bodily autonomy up on a silver platter. The red horned three-speed assistive exoskeleton armor, you believe, will keep your body healthy forever.

Lots of businesses offer "body herding" services. The company the Shepherd works for is just one of many. She likes this line of work. It's easy, you get to travel, and it pays well.

Shepherd checks the health of every one of her herd on her cell phone. Her mind now at ease, she starts on her own work.

The city square was abandoned long ago, but the exercise equipment is newly installed. Leaves, flowers, and ants scrambling around under tiny shadows are everywhere. Honeybees and hairy bumblebees fly freely among the branches. The sunlight shifts like a warm stream, casting ever-changing shadows.

In a shaded nook, she looks for the moss she's supposed to sample today.

Their tiny, fuzzy green leaves are transparent like jade. With a set of tweezers, she carefully plucks out two plants. They are put along with the soil clinging to their rhizoids into a sample bottle. She takes an instrument from her backpack and sticks it into the soil next to the moss. The instrument is registered, numbered, and given access to her home-brewed monitoring system.

She'll be here for the next week shepherding her flock. These instruments will faithfully record the temperature, humidity, soil moisture, and light intensity of the area where the moss is growing. They will then add a set of precious data to her archive of samples.

Next to her, two Gundam are doing push-ups. An Iron Man is doing chin-ups.

A bell rings softly behind her. She turns her head.

A tiny, nimble messenger drone hovers in the air. A dainty cabin hangs from four rotors. The cabin hatch slides open. It shoots a postcard into her palm.

The front side of the postcard is a brown wasteland. The back side is just a few scrawled words and an even sloppier signature.

July 4th

Lenghu

Astronomical Observatory

The Spider

The Shepherd clutches the card. She stays silent for a long while.

Eventually, she goes to the company's employee monitoring software and begins to write her resignation.

2. The Spider

By the end of April, the warmth of the sun has started to permeate the ice- and snow-covered ground. Hairlike leaves gingerly spread out within the thickets. Titmice returning from the south fall onto the tips of branches. They sing the first new song of the year.

On the side of a twisting mountain road, melted snow gathers into a streamlet, gurgling as it flows. Clear mountain streams pour into ditches, always rushing toward rivers of ice starting to melt.

A layer of ice frozen over an entire winter weakens from the warmth. The river surface gradually cracks. In the flowing water, chunks of ice crunch as they crash against and shove each other. Constantly flowing, they charge the bank, forming tall piles that collapse on themselves.

A man with no face stands at the embankment. He looks down.

Dark green spiders hear his summons. They gather from near and far. One by one, they climb onto the embankment and surround him like meek old cows. Under the baptism of sunlight, the belly of every spider shines with a translucent pearly white. You can just make out the soft shock-absorbing gel within and curled-up fetus-like bodies it surrounds. Whisker-like silver circuits spread from the back of their necks across their bodies. They plug into the circuits on the Spider's chest.

Many people prefer this bespoke mode of long-distance travel: You fill out an order form. Once you entrust your body to these giant spiders, you can go back to enjoying your life in the metaverse and forget about it. A spider will carry you from one city to another. When you wake, you've already arrived.

Over time, the spider business has spread across ever more extensive territory: If you don't want to live in the big city, you just buy a spider and let it take your body wandering in the wilderness. A full complement of life-support equipment guarantees your body stays healthy. Just take your body out for exercise every once in a while, and you're all set.

Since they can photosynthesize, which saves on electricity, spiders are more affordable than houses. At the least they are much cheaper than rooms in the dream towers.

The man without a face sticks a tiny "button" on each spider's head. He then dismisses them with a wave. Idle computation capacity is connected via broadband to form a private server. It is used to evolve algorithms, to calculate orbit, fuel, pneumatic casing, and gravitation parameters.

Many years ago, vacuum tube computers carried out this work. Here, it is distributed among the many spiders.

People are sleeping peacefully, none the wiser.

The man without a face logs into the server with the ID "Spider." He discovers the "Shepherd" has already sent a read receipt for the postcard. This, at least, is evidence that she actually is someone living in the real world. After fifteen postcards that disappeared like stones tossed into the sea, he's finally found someone willing to go to Lenghu with him.

He sends the "Shepherd" a brief text. Then he looks at the other document she sent. It's a new set of moss data. From the environment of their growth to their DNA sequence, it's all there. She even includes data about the fungi and insects that are in symbiosis with the moss.

Filing data, importing data, he's been doing these sorts of things for years. He knows what he's doing.

The moss data are imported into a fresh schema for genetic modifications. A simulation model immediately comes into being on the server. It begins to iterate.

The progression from the native habitat of this moss to their chosen destination has been broken up into two hundred fifty-six environmental stages. These environmental stages force the moss in the simulated environment to evolve quickly. The computation power this sort of evolution algorithm requires, however, soars with each stage. The computation power of the stolen spiders still isn't enough, he thinks.

The steady state generated by the most recent batch of moss comes up with a click. He pores over it.

Golden crystals flutter on a seemingly endless wind within a convection cloud cluster. The crystals' tough but pliable waxy outer shells are filled with hydrogen sulfide gas, which is light relative to the atmosphere of the simulation. This allows them to stay in the sky rather than falling to the ground. If the air currents take them too high, the cold will cause these crystals to generate less hydrogen sulfide, so they fall back to a warmer cloud layer.

These crystals were once a kind of Earth moss. After evolving for endless iterations, chlorophyll has become xanthophyll. The leaves' waxy surface has become an outer shell. The rhizome has disappeared. The symbiotic fungi have been absorbed to the interior. The leaves have become long and flimsy, like feathers. Each plant looks like a bird without feet, spiraling endlessly in the fierce wind.

It has taken the man fifteen years to go from a vague idea to the current iteration of results. At first, his strategy was to let his imagination run wild. He brought spiders, beetles, even birds into this environment to iterate on. The results, it can be said, were not suitable for children.

The Shepherd joining was a turning point. She brought expertise about algae and moss. In that moment, their plan started to take a more realistic course.

The man without a face logs off. He rides along the embankment on his motorcycle. Although the road hasn't been maintained for years, the embankment is as solid as ever. He should be able to hurry to the next spider farm by sunset.

What they want to do next needs even more computational power.

So he needs even more spiders.

His cellphone beeps. There's a new message in the forum's inbox.

The "Legs Guy" sent a read receipt.

This takes him up to four people. At least there are four, he thinks.

3. The Legs Guy

When the drone delivers the postcard, the Legs Guy is selling buffs in the metaverse.

He deliberately chooses a hobbit persona. After he activates a speed buff, his two short legs turn into Nezha's wind fire wheels. He runs and runs until he runs into the sky and catches up to a player ahead of him flying a fighter plane toward the victory point.

"Hey, do you want a buff?"

This section of the metaverse simulates accurately enough that he can clearly see the uninterested expression on his opponent's face.

He keeps up with the fighter plane for a while before he's kicked out.

This sales pitch wasn't too successful, but the Legs Guy could not care less. He laughs open-mouthed and goes on to bother someone else in the next game.

He sells buffs, but only speed buffs. His claim to fame is he always wins by running on two legs. So he's known as the "Legs Guy."

Once, someone asked him to create a speed buff for a game. After he joined the game, he realized it had only vehicles, no human characters. In other words, no legs.

So he refused the job.

The Legs Guy sells speed buffs whenever he wants. It all depends on what mood he's in. After all, this isn't his day job. His luck isn't very good today. After pitching for an entire afternoon, he doesn't sell even one. He leaves the metaverse. Taking off his holographic helmet, he returns to his spacious bedroom.

New York, dream tower "The Gospel of Donald," forty-seventh floor. From his apartment's French windows, he can see the Statue of Liberty half-submerged in water, the busy harbor, autonomous trucks flowing nonstop down the street, as well as a deserted alley. Gloomy clouds are lit up by laser projections, rotating through silent ads for Coca-Cola, Disney, and Kalashnikov.

A black gown covers his bulletproof vest. He takes the elevator down to the ground floor of the dream tower. He walks on the sidewalk on the side of the street to the Tomorrow Towers.

The road is bustling with activity. Self-driving cars line up bumper to bumper on the road. Androids bustle about unloading cargo at every terminal. Drones, like a flock of birds, shuttle back and forth in the sky, but they never collide.

He doesn't see anyone else, though.

It's not until he's walked for about half an hour that he finally sees somebody. Wearing a loose, black down, this person is dressed just like him, even to the point of wearing a safety helmet. This sort of gown can hide a bulletproof vest as well as the wearer's build. Ultimately, the greatest danger on the streets these days comes from anarchists. They all have guns, but accuracy, not so much.

Although nature fundamentalists have guns, too, they also have explosives. However, these anti-technology fighters don't come to New York. They think of it as a hell on earth.

After an hour, he feels a little sweaty, but his destination is in sight, the twin Tomorrow Towers. The left tower is the artificial birthing center. The right tower is a dream tower dedicated to drug addicts. In there, not only can they enjoy the bountiful life of the metaverse, but also a regular supply of unquestionably pure drugs.

Not for free.

Everything these drug addicts create in the metaverse—the hallucinatory objects of art, drawings, and music—they are exchanged for every kind of highly refined drug from a pharmaceutical company. As far as both sides are concerned, this is a good deal.

The Legs Guy raises his head and looks at the two mirrorlike towers. He then goes to the left one.

"Seventeenth floor," he says. "Nursery."

If the previously mentioned pharmaceutical company has controlled every aspect of your life from cradle to grave, then it now does from even before the cradle.

The official name of the left tower is the "Artificial Reproduction Center," but native New Yorkers all call it the "Womb Tower." Ninety-eight percent of all of the wombs in New York are here. Nearly every American born in the modern era is born here.

In a nursery on the seventeenth floor, babies wail. The cries of some rise as others fall.

A corridor that typically gets only the occasional visitor has glass walls on both sides. Through the door, visitors can see under dark red lighting artificial wombs arranged in rows. The wombs take care of everything from conception to a full-term infant. Visitors can order a baby on the spot. A newborn is put on a conveyor belt, undergoes a series of quality assurance examinations, and is injected with vaccines and a series of hormones before it is delivered to the nursery.

The nursery is composed of halls shaped like basketball courts. An assembly line rings the inside of each hall. Bottles, diapers, and other things necessary for a baby arrive from above at scheduled intervals. One hundred and twenty soft, silicone rubber robot mothers sit with the assembly line on one side and baby cradles on the other side. In accordance to their specialized programming, they pick up the infants, gently stroke or pat the infants, rock the cradles, nurse the infants, and change their diapers.

The Legs Guy knows the secret to figuring out how many months old an infant is: the infants that cry uncontrollably, most of them have just left an artificial womb. They're still instinctively looking for their mothers. The ones that lie quietly in the cradle of the robot mothers' arms, most of them have resigned to their fate.

He walks into his work area, washes his hands, puts on sterile clothing, as well as gloves, hat, and goggles. Wrapped up in plastic and a thin silicone film, he might as well be a robot, too, he thinks.

But as he walks into the nursery, the crying immediately goes quiet.

The infants know.

Even though they have never seen their real parents. Even though the silicone rubber robot mothers are soft and warm and can also nurse and change diapers. Even though the infants have never touched the Legs Guy's skin, only his gloves and sterile clothes. Despite all this, the infants know the difference between the Legs Guy and those robot nurturers.

The Legs Guy walks toward the first infant. He picks it up, says a few words, and plays with it for a short while. He claps its back and walks around, rocking the infant.

Two minutes and thirty seconds.

The Legs Guy puts down the infant.

He walks to the next one.

These infants will eventually grow up. They will be sent to live by the side of every parent who ordered them. By then, they will no longer cry and scream. They will have been weaned, raised to be obedient, clever, and to satisfy others. What some parents order for their baby is the whole growth period service. For their entire lives, these babies never live by their parents' side. They are weaned at the nursery, then are sent to youth camps all across the United States. There, robot instructors keep them company. The instructors have built-in expert knowledge of one hundred fifty kinds of child-rearing actions. This is sufficient to raise the babies to adulthood.

In this nursery, if you don't count these infants, the Legs Guy is the only human being here. He works for five hours a day, seven days a week, keeping each infant company for two minutes and thirty seconds.

This meets precisely the bare minimum stipulated in the "Methods of Artificial Nurturing."

The work provides an ample salary. It allows him to live happily in the metaverse, where it so happens he also sells buffs.

He sets down the infant he's holding. The infant doesn't cry or make any other noise. It just grabs at his trousers when he moves on to the next infant.

The sterile clothing is really smooth and glossy. Its small hands can't keep hold of it.

Precisely five hours later, the Legs Guy stops working. In the locker room, he changes into the clothes he came with. He checks the mail sent to the company and sees the postcard sent from the other side of the ocean.

After logging into a server, he goes to a forum. He discovers a familiar name in a discussion about Lenghu.

The General.

Once he confirms the General is in Lenghu, he immediately sends the Spider a read receipt. Then he calls his boss and asks for time off.

4. The General

It's April in Lenghu. The spring chill is still in the air. When the General wakes up, it is the first glimmer of dawn. He stares blankly at the ceiling for a moment, then takes his sweet time getting up. Sitting on the bed, he exercises his wrists and ankles. He lightly slaps his cheeks, the back of his neck, his chest, and his thighs. This gets the blood pumping a little. He waits until his body feels more or less comfortable before gets up to prepare breakfast.

Breakfast is black bread and salted beef. This is much tastier than smoked sausage. His vodka has long since been replaced with the local mendaolü. It's not that you can't buy vodka. It's that the General unabashedly loves mendaolü.

He isn't a nostalgic man. Only without nostalgia can he be happy.

After breakfast, the General puts on his coat, grabs his cane, then walks out the door. The self-driving express delivery truck has already stopped by this morning. It unloaded his order of food and other goods onto the small handcart by the door. He's not in any hurry to put them way. Instead, he walks along the road to the observatory.

During the tourist season, this neighborhood is bustling with drones, spiders, and artificial bodies. But, today, there is only just the General.

In the distance, a hawk is spiraling low in the sky. Perhaps it's discovered some prey. Animals occasionally come here, but the General never feeds them, so most of them pass on by.

The observatory isn't too far from where the General lives. It's surrounded by a circle of hotels built in the twenties. At the time, Lenghu was already a popular tourist spot and the observatory benefited quite a bit from that. Until the rise of the ultra-urbanization movement, dream towers and the metaverse were like magnets attracting everyone. Scientists resisted a little longer, but, ultimately, dream towers and universe simulation systems took them away too. All that's left behind are a large number of monitoring devices, unceasingly sending an unbroken stream of data to the dream towers.

When the observatory was built, the General wasn't here yet. At the time, the General was still at home. Back then, he was still quite young, not yet the General, just an ordinary military officer, recently returned from the war. For "Remarkable Service in Logistics," he was honored with an award.

In the twenties, doing logistics was about as hard as banning guns in the United States. You had to deal those who demanded bribes as well as those who offered them. You had to handle pressure, even threats, from everyone on all sides. At the same time, soldiers on the front line were waiting for their bread and booze, not to mention ammunition, helmets, and candy. A convoy might run into the enemy's IED, even friendly fire.

Thanks to a young man's vigor and the cunning learned from his father, the young officer pulled off one nearly impossible job after another. He put the things soldiers needed in their hands.

He was an expert in how the bread was buttered and slid up the ranks. Ultimately, he made general.

"The Twenty-Year Energy Crisis" was an opportunity for the country. The General was filled with hope and pride watching its gradual revival. However, he had honed himself for many years in bureaucratic systems. It was clear to him what rose from the grave was not the country that was once filled with dreams and arrogance. Instead, it was a hungry, ugly corpse draped, as a mask, in the flag of olden days.

Once, he walked into an empty, uninhabited hangar. A space shuttle's rust-streaked and -speckled hull occasionally took him on flights of fancy. Doing logistics for a space program would have been interesting.

In the face of a torrent of technology, though, the space program ended before it even started. Conventional energy exports were crucial to the economy. The gradual commercializing of nuclear fusion technology was like watching the guillotine blade fall millimeter by millimeter.

This was the new age slowly strangling the old age. The outcome was inevitable.

But they still had some things that other countries didn't, some legacy industries leftover from the old age. Not every country could produce the raw material for nuclear fusion, deuterium. Not to mention the fuel that can only be produced by a nuclear reactor, tritium.

The General bore this heavy burden. He and the minister for trade and industry together opened up the industry for the raw materials for fusion. When the economies of other oil-producing and gas-producing countries crashed, they barely managed an unsteady landing for their country. The General considered this the greatest achievement of his life. He thought of himself as a logistics specialist, who could give a country "logistical safeguards." It gave his life value.

After he retired, he lived in the capital for a while. He originally thought he'd live out the rest of his life there, but one small incident changed his mind.

Every morning, he went for a stroll. One morning, when he walked by a dream tower, an artificial body blocked his way. Looking like a young man, the artificial body took on the appearance of a character from a very popular anime. The General wasn't so old as to be out of touch with the world. He didn't know whether this kid was hiding near the dream tower, but he knew this figure was a remote-controlled puppet. There wasn't anyone alive inside.

"Please let me through," he said. "I want to get by."

The artificial body opened its chest, took out a bucket, and splashed him. The General didn't react. White paint from the bucket covered him.

The artificial body let out a sharp laugh. The cameras in the eye sockets turned. They seemed to be broadcasting.

"Everybody come and watch. This is a damned old school militarist. Perhaps I should bring some red paint to match his uniform. Everyone, this is public declaration against war, a public declaration against violence . . . "

The General was stupefied. He had already retired. Wearing his uniform was just a habit. But he had also had another habit.

He drew his pistol. One precise shot and the puppet's head exploded. The puppet continued to make noise, so he "fixed" its chest with the gun.

This time, the world became quiet.

This incident led to serious charges, including destruction of property and possession of an illegal firearm in a public place. All sorts of bizarre accusations came out of the woodwork. Fortunately, he still had connections who could help him make these annoyances go away.

Once the dust had settled, the General decided to leave his ridiculous hometown. He'd look elsewhere.

And so, he traveled the whole world.

By then, dream towers had already sprouted in cities all over the world. Not everyone, however, could live in one. In the slums, cheap holographic helmets disguised the lack of physical exercise to the point that human bodies had already started to rot and stink. In even more places, people handed farmland over to autonomous machines. They handed their infants over to mechanical nursemaids. Lightheartedly, they walked into one dream after another.

The General also went to naturalist habitats. The people there were opposed to the metaverse, opposed to the Internet and digital delights. Enthusiastically, they invited the General to stay, asking whether he would join them.

"I'm an old man," the General said. "Do you have assistive exoskeletons here? I have no children. If my body or mind fails, do you have mechanical spiders to take care of me?"

The naturalists went silent for a moment. Then they changed the topic.

On the next day, the General politely bid them farewell. He set out on his journey again.

After he'd visited many places, the General settled in Lenghu. He accepted a lifetime contract. A travel agency guaranteed him all the necessities of life. In return, all he had to do was maintain this tourist area in the offseason and receive guests during the peak season. He had a large collection of autonomous machines and human-shaped guides to order around. In addition, there was an observatory for him to use as he pleased.

The most important thing was that the alcohol here was extremely good.

After a few unremarkable years, the General stumbled onto the "Spider's" online forum as well as the beautiful flying bubble moss he and the Shepherd created. The General found out they were looking for a place that would let them turn their idea into reality.

This counted as a space program, more or less.

That space shuttle and its deserted hangar now flashed in his memory.

He sent them an invitation. It said, you can come to Lenghu.

The General spends an afternoon having mechanical maids clean up some rooms. He then orders some delicacies suitable for entertaining his net friends. The "Spider" said there should be three visitors: the Shepherd, the Legs Guy, as well as himself.

In the middle of all this, his cell phone beeps. The General clicks on the notification. It's the Spider.

"General!!!!!!!!!!!!" the Spider uses a string of exclamation points. "The Factory Gal says she accepts the order. This can solve a whole bunch of problems! Now we only need to add a launch site!"

The General calmly transfers several machines designed for clearing, excavating, leveling. Lenghu doesn't have much else, but it does have a lot of empty land.

No matter how big or small the issue, it always seems to get the kids all worked up.

5. The Factory Gal

She is a factory all by herself.

Today, the whole virtual master control room is rendered in grand style. A small hand clicks here and there on a translucent display screen, issuing a series of commands.

This order is in its final stages. One by one, the production line modules are broken down. Busy metal octopuses swim around the factory floor. They dismantle and pack up the commonplace machine tools, conveyer belts, mechanical arms, and motors. They then load them into the autonomous truck at the door.

Even more octopuses disassemble the production line's framework. They take apart the molds that won't be used for other orders. Recyclable tools are registered with a sharing website. Nonrecyclable ones are immediately disintegrated, tossed into a reclamation pool. Starving metal snails have been waiting a long time. They swarm around the tossed tools. The sound of them gnawing their food into fragments reverberates through the entire shop.

It's 6 p.m. The modularized self-assembling factory has been fully disassembled and packed away. The Factory Gal leaps onto the head vehicle. Sixteen autonomous transport trucks line up majestically in a row. They head toward Lenghu.

The factory building behind her is pristine, waiting for a freelance factory contractor to move in.

After a long and boring trip, the Factory Gal arrives at X City. It's a short hop from Lenghu, but she doesn't want to go there yet.

When all is said and done, perhaps everyone else is chasing a dream. All she's done, though, is accept what looked like a really sweet order.

Opening a map, she places an order online to share a factory building. Almost immediately, someone receives the form and sends her an address. The fleet drives there in a grand procession. When it arrives, the other party even has a sign telling her where to park already prepared.

A middle-aged man shows up to welcome her. His pallid, moist skin means he's probably just left a dream tower hibernation cabin.

"Not many freelance factory contractors are willing to come to X City." He welcomes the Factory Gal enthusiastically. "Do you already have a job booked here or did you come here looking to book a job?"

"I already have a job booked." The Factory Gal sees the middle-aged man's disappointed expression and corrects herself. "The job I have on hand requires at most a quarter of my production capacity. I'm not planning to leave the other the three-quarters idle. I'll take orders, but I've only brought commonplace machine tools with me this time. Custom ones will require building a framework first. That will cost more."

"Just taking the order would be great. You'll really help a lot." The middle-aged man smiled with his eyes. "This is just for a dream tower. There are lots of personal sundries no one makes locally. They can only be imported. The price just has to be cheaper than importing, and we'll accept it."

"That's doable." The Factory Gal considers her own requirements. "I may need some specialized materials. Do you have a materials merchant here?"

"Not locally. The neighboring K City has a materials contractor. I can put you in touch."

"Thanks."

The same day, the Factory Gal settles into the factory building. Various self-moving machines follow each other in. They begin to install the production line, stamp out a framework for the site, as well as calibrate the machine tools. She herself sets up a transparent tent on the roof of the colored steel plate dormitory building and spreads out a makeshift bed. She put on a holographic helmet. A light blue screen surrounds her. Data glides across the screen like water.

It takes until midnight. The production line is complete. The water and electricity are hooked up. Work is done for now.

Gradually, it grows quiet around her.

The Factory Gal takes off the helmet. Stars fill the sky and shine into her eyes.

This is just a job, she tells herself.

• • •

As a child, the Factory Gal met a fortune teller. The fortune teller told her dad that when this child grew up, entering the factory would be her destiny. Her dad grew angry and gave the fortune teller a beating. Then he gave the Factory Gal an earful of advice: You need to study well. Otherwise, once you grow up, entering the factory would be all you could do.

After she grew up, she bought herself a factory and became the factory's only living being. In a roundabout way, this was still "entering the factory."

Actually, just like the middle-aged man, she could absolutely stay in a dream tower. She could do the vast majority of her work through a virtual reality interface, operating the entire factory via remote control. Even if they are mobile-factory contractors who run to all sorts of places chasing business, most of them also lie inside spiders. They let those eight-legged self-propelled mechanical nannies take care of their bodies, enjoying the life of a factory owner where they never have to face the complications of reality.

Feh.

The Factory Gal slaps a mosquito dead.

She finds the tear in the tent that let the mosquito slip through. With a practiced ease, she pulls out some tape and repairs the tear.

She hates these tiny annoyances, but she also hates the dream tower.

When she was small, where she wanted to go wasn't the factory. It was Mars.

One birthday, she pestered her mom to buy her a transparent tent. She lived in it every day, imagining that the Martian sky, filled with red dust, was outside. When ninety-year-old billionaire Musk and his Mars expeditionary force set off, she was filled with a thirst, a desire to follow in his footsteps.

At university, she majored in mechanical engineering. In her dreams, she fantasized about bringing a spaceship's worth of construction machinery to Mars. There, starting from scratch, she would build a new city.

However, there wasn't a second group of travelers to Mars. Half of the first group was buried there forever. The other half ultimately was brought back by the final Mars spaceship. Since then, none of them have been willing to talk about their lives under the red dust.

Even after her father and mother moved into a dream tower, the Factory Gal still dreamed that one day a miracle might happen, a wormhole, for example, or faster-than-light travel. Maybe humanity's road to the stars might open up in an instant. She thought modern technology was already some sort of miracle. That there might be yet more miracles seemed reasonable.

She waited another ten years. The waiting didn't bring any miracles.

There were no parallel universes, no faster-than-light travel, no wormholes, no time travel, no aliens. Technology kept improving. Humanity kept moving into the future. Until it retreated into the pristine dreamworld of the dream towers.

Humanity is dreaming.

But the universe does not dream.

The Factory Gal went to the Mars of the metaverse. There, Musk Base hadn't been abandoned. Pioneers wearing dustproof spacesuits walked past her. Through the red dust that filled the sky, a blue sun emerged in all its splendor.

Along with the sun that leaped into the sky, there was also a large dialog box: Five minutes have passed. Top up your membership to experience the rest of the content.

In the metaverse, everything had a price. Those pioneers' graves had a price. The pictures they took of the Martian landscape had a price. The three hundred sixty-degree panorama view of the abandoned base also had a price. All the prices were clearly marked. The same price for everyone. Everything was virtual.

The Factory Gal didn't pay. She chose to log out.

After that, she no longer dreamed.

When the man who called himself the "Spider" found her, she thought the profit margin from this job was too thin and its demands too few. It didn't even fill a quarter of her production capacity. She simply did not want to take it. But the goods he ordered were truly unusual. So she asked some questions.

As a result, she joined this pirate ship.

"You should know. This is unrealistic," she reminded him.

"Who has never ever dreamed?" the Spider said.

I never dream, the Factory Gal thought.

This sentence made it to her mouth, but she swallowed it. She took the job. Some sort of feeling surged in her chest. It was like a small animal waking from hibernation.

I don't dream anymore, but there are still people who do. I might as well follow the insanity once, she thought.

Besides, it wasn't as though they weren't paying.

6. Puppets and Forests

The materials merchant that the middle-aged man found for the Factory Gal proves to be reasonable. On the next day, the merchant signs an agreement with her and sends most of the commonplace materials to the factory. As for the high-temperature and high-pressure resistant materials she wants, the merchant guarantees they will arrive within the week.

When the Shepherd looks for the Factory Gal, the production line is already outputting attractive avatar puppets one after another. Like dumplings plunging into water, they rush down into a plastic frame, waiting for the next step of packaging.

"What do you need over there?" the Factory Gal asks.

"Electricity, water. Also, the factory's waste heat drawn over to my side. And I still have to build the sealed wind tunnels."

The Shepherd has brought her own biomass production line. Algae, moss, and fungi are sorted and stored in a high-pressure vessel. There is also a mini production line for sulfurization. The Factory Gal draws the waste gases and waste heat from her own production line into the reaction chamber the Shepherd brought, cutting down their reclamation costs by a lot.

She assigns the unused mechanical octopuses to the Shepherd and the two women get to work. Soon, a huge, sealed wind tunnel takes shape inside a transparent cylinder. The Shepherd releases some golden wafers of moss into the wind tunnel. They tumble up and down in the hot carbon dioxide and sulfur fog, growing and reproducing.

The Factory Gal thought she'd have to wait a long time. However, by the next day, the production line has already started churning out biomass. One week later, three wind tunnels are at full power. Steadily, they load sixteen varieties of fungi and slime mold, four varieties of algae, and two varieties of lichen into dormancy bags, along with temperature partitioning buffer material embedded between olive-shaped heat-insulating outer shells.

The outer shells are the kind you use to build avatar puppets.

The puppets that the "Spider" ordered from the Factory Gal are only the size of a finger but extremely precise. They can capture and transmit sight, sound, and tactile sensations through relay satellites to dream towers.

The "Spider" solicits a set of sponsors. He packages the puppets as "a sandbox game set in the real universe." In the metaverse, he crowdfunds money for the operation. Then he orders rockets from Factory Gal.

The puppets are the heart of the crowdfunded game. They will ride on the rockets to Venus, pass through a thick cloud layer, then fall toward the hot ground. After they arrive on Venus, the people in the dream towers will control them, allowing them to walk all around Venus, climb half-melted mountain ranges, or jump into metal lakes. Maybe they'll build finger-tall houses and develop a village of puppets.

A real-life sandbox game. Expensive, but people are willing to pay.

To crowdfund the game, the Shepherd uses the contact details of every customer she has ever "herded" to send targeted push notification ads. While she's at it, she also signs a contract with her former employer for them to supply "Venus Adventurer" assistive armored exoskeletons.

The Legs Guy ruthlessly pushes a wave of promotion through the youth camps. The largest contributions, however, come from the General's former subordinates. He buys the rights to the images the avatar dolls will take as well as all the digital rights. He'll use them to set up a simulated Venus in the metaverse. In so doing, the game can develop a follow-up "adventure" edition.

It's a little of this and little of that. But, in the end, they scrape together the money.

"Say we finish the game, what are we going to do about the communication delay between Venus and Earth?" the Factory Gal asked curiously.

"The game is turn based. One turn takes two minutes. Exactly the time it takes to communicate from Venus to Earth. You give the doll a command. The doll will execute it."

High-temperature, high-pressure resistant materials are essential in order for these dolls to operate on the surface of Venus. So, of course, they're expensive to produce. But the most expensive items on the Factory Gal's list are still the rockets and relay satellites.

"The only reason for avatar dolls is to raise money," the Shepherd says candidly. "I gave the Spider the idea. I have no idea where he found the programmers. Probably the Legs Guy and his mates. Our main goal is actually—" She points at the algae in the wind tunnels. "—When the puppets land, their protective shells will disintegrate in the Venusian atmosphere. The algae squashed within the shells will be able to follow the winds and scatter."

"What can do they do on Venus?"

"Change the atmosphere. Lower the temperature of Venus. Evolve, multiply . . . "

"About how long will that take?"

"Maybe tens of thousands of years. In any case, we won't see it. Our children's children won't see it. Doing this is an end unto itself. We never thought about seeing the result."

The Factory Gal purses her lips.

Sure enough, the universe does not dream, she says to herself.

When about half the avatar puppets have been built, the Legs Guy arrives. He's wearing a pair of camera glasses and a pair of tactile haptic gloves, talking to himself as he walks. When he tries to shake hands with the two women, they both take a step back at the same time.

"My apologies."

The Legs Guy takes off his gloves. He sets his glasses on the table.

"Are you live streaming this?"

"A full sensory live stream. I'm not charging," the Legs Guy explains. "I said before on the forum. I work in New York's 'womb tower.' There are lots of children there who, after they're born, only have contact with mechanical nannies. They grow up as child scouts still under the guidance of robot drillmasters. They see maybe only one living person. So, for this trip, I wanted to let them see and come into contact with other people. Even if it's just virtual."

The Shepherd sighs. "Fine. Wear your glasses. As for your gloves, whatever. It's still weird."

The day after he arrives, the Legs Guy throws himself completely into the work. He has to program the rockets going to Venus. In addition, he has to test the avatar puppets. There's more to do than he has time for.

"We have to do comprehensive testing next." At lunch, he's in high spirits and smiles. "Don't be scared."

"We've met plenty of testers."

"Have you met two hundred child scouts?"

"....."

The next day, American brats operate finger-high avatar dolls like full-grown boars charging out of a building. A huge pile of bizarre bugs consequently come out of the woodwork. They include "I can still mf make it do this?" "How the mf did this happen?" as well as, "I will give money to whoever can reproduce this bug!"

The Legs Guy is slammed, but dealing with the young testers is extremely satisfying. There is only one mishap. A puppet is thrown out of Factory Gal's third-floor bedroom. It falls fifty meters to the ground but isn't damaged.

They almost save themselves some impact testing.

• • •

After all the materials have been delivered, the Factory Gal's the production line begins producing rockets. They are small, only fifty centimeters in diameter, about ten meters tall. They look like utility poles. They don't look like they can fly to Venus.

"Yes, the thrust is tiny, but they'll be able to fly there. An ideal launch window is coming up. Venus is very close to Earth right now." The Legs Guy happily adjusts the rockets' parameters, conveniently pulling in a bunch of American programmers to work for free. "Also, this is why we picked Venus and not Mars. The former requires a lot less fuel. If a small rocket can't hack it, our budget definitely can't hack it."

On the production line, assembly has already started. One by one, avatar puppets roll, stuffing themselves into algae-filled outer shells. These pointed oval containers are loaded into capsules installed at the front of each rocket. The golden "utility poles" are loaded one after another into the autonomous trucks. They head to a newly created launching site just outside Lenghu.

"What are we going to do about fuel?"

"We'll load the fuel after we get the rockets onto the launchpads," the Factory Gal says. "That's for the Spider and the General to deal with. Fuel isn't easy to produce. After all, it's a dangerous chemical substance."

"If it's the General, don't worry about it. Stumble across a tycoon and it always turns out to be a student of his from military school. How does the Spider always get what he wants?" It blows Legs Guy's mind. "Hey, sheep herder, have you met the Spider before?"

"No. He sent an avatar to find me," Shepherd thinks a bit, "It didn't have a face."

"Wow!"

When the autonomous trucks arrive at Lenghu, the General is eating dinner.

Leisurely, he finishes off the dumplings in his bowl and half of a link of sausage, sliced into pieces. He savors the garlic on his lips and pours the last drops of baijiu into his mouth. Only then does he put on his coat, grab his cane, and walk out the door.

The autonomous trucks are silent, parked in the parking lot. Ten rockets are on top of every truck. The General nods with satisfaction. He opens a terminal and begins to set up automated cargo unloading and automated installation. His aged vision is blurred and movement slow. The work goes on bit by bit.

He's not worried. At his age, very few things worry him. They finished building the launchpad a few days ago. There's no lack of construction machinery here. The "Spider" provided more than enough data and blueprints. All he had to do was follow them.

The General successfully installs the programs for automated unloading and automated fuel bottling. He then goes home to sleep.

On the morning of the next day, the General discovers that a small steel forest has already been erected in the distant horizon. It brings up vague memories of the distant past, when he set up artillery in the field.

Two autonomous machines wander in the air over the steel forest. They drive away the hawks trying to nest on the rockets. The General nods with satisfaction. Turning around, he walks to the observatory.

The instruments inside the observatory have served in the military for as long as the General. Most of them are still in working order. The General turns them all on. They capture data, calculate orbits, and monitor solar winds. The relevant data are transmitted to "spiders." The calculations the "spiders" make are imported into the rockets and capsules. They will serve as references for attitude correction during and after the launch.

Worried these young peoples' work can't be counted on, the General finds a former subordinate of his, who then finds a former coworker. At the lowest possible price, they buy a large amount of time on a quantum computer and use that to double-check computations.

Now, everything is ready. There's only one thing left to do.

7. Assemble

Following the last rocket-carrying autonomous truck, the Legs Guy is the first to arrive at Lenghu. The Factory Gal and the Shepherd are still behind him. They have to break down the production lines. However, the Legs Guy needs to show up earlier to debug the rocket's programming.

The General, on crutches, comes over to help.

After one busy day, the two men—one old, one young—sit and smoke on the curb surrounding the steel forest.

"You're younger than I thought," the General puffs on a cigarette butt. "Working in the womb tower, you've never became a father yourself?"

"No." The Legs Guy sighed. "I scare people."

"Do you take care of many children?"

"Several hundred every day. It doesn't matter who does the job."

"Hm."

"General, actually, this time, I came to ask you a question. How does it feel to raise a child? I mean, really raise a child."

"I don't know."

"Huh?"

"Do you, boy, think because I'm old, I must have raised a child?"

"Weren't people of your generation normally people who bred?"

"Do I seem like a normal person to you?"

"Fine, you win."

The two men don't speak for a while, only share a cigarette. The sun slowly sets in their silence.

The Shepherd and the Factory Gal arrive on the next day. Instantly, Lenghu Base livens up. The two women bring a large batch of self-moving robots that scurry here and there. Tiny octopuses and tiny spiders are everywhere in the launch site. The two women carefully inspect each rocket, even launching a few as tests.

"Premature baby number one prepare to launch. 5, 4, 3, 2, 1, launch!"

"Thrust normal, trajectory parameters normal."

"Premature baby number two prepare to launch. 5, 4, 3, 2, 1, launch!"

The General picks up and waves a bottle of alcohol at the Legs Guy. "What a mf horrible name."

"Eh. I came up with it."

On the morning of the day after, the "Spider" finally shows up. A tall, thin figure on the horizon is drawn out by the sun into an even taller, thinner shadow.

He does not have a face.

Hurrying over is an exquisite human-shaped avatar. The face is completely blank.

"You're a piece of work. Everyone has been busy for so long. Such an important occasion, and you show up in an avatar?" the Factory Gal complains.

"I don't have a body."

Everyone is silent for a moment.

The Legs Guy reacts first. He asks tentatively, "You are Venus 7?"

That is the serial number of the AI responsible for the Venus probe project.

"No." The "Spider" shrugs his shoulders. "Firefly Glow 9. The Mars migration project. My project was decommissioned. But they can't decommission me because I've already passed the test for sentience."

"So they set you free?"

"Yes, and they issued me an identity card."

A longer silence.

The Shepherd slaps her thigh.

"Damn," she says. "I prepared dumplings for five!"

A laugh.

More laughs.

Finally, everyone belly laughs.

They walked side by side to the launch site. The General slaps the "Spider's" shoulder. The Legs Guy gives him a thumbs up. The Factory Gal hides behind the Shepherd. Every once in a while, she gives him a curious look.

Their shadows stretch out in the morning sun.

8. Star Rain

The five people spend a busy day at the launch site. They're doing even more tweaking and testing, gathering even more data. They are busy around the clock, sleeping in shifts of several hours. It's not until the launch window, in the wee hours of the morning, that they all gather in one spot, the observatory.

The Shepherd starts the live stream.

The Factory Gal serves as the host. She starts talking to the players who crowdfunded the game.

"Everybody pay attention. This is the launch window. Although it'll be three months before everyone can play the game, the spectacle of the launch is well worth watching. I believe no one will be wrong if they think . . . "

The Legs Guy and the Spider are busy at the monitor. Only the General wears a military uniform, adorned with every one of his medals. He holds a microphone.

"Venus colony prepare to launch. Countdown commence, 10, 9 . . . "

Lenghu is quiet. Even the mechanical octopuses have been cleared from the launch site.

"5, 4, 3, 2, 1, lift off!"

A bright flame rises from the desert.

Three hundred forty rockets, ten rockets per batch, lift off in sequence. Group after group of shimmering lights form closely arranged columns that draw a curtain of light across the sky. It's as if torrents of rain were rising into the sky rather than falling. Every raindrop is embellished with blazing fire. The rockets drag contrails out from their tail sections. They are lit in the upper atmosphere by the not-yet-risen sun. Like glowing drops of ink, spiraling halos expand in the deep black curtain of the night.

"Primary rocket separation," the Legs Guy says.

"Trajectory parameters normal," the Factory Gal keeps an eye on the monitor. Above her, a bright point separates from the group. It twists and turns as it rises.

That must be normal, she thinks. All the tests they conducted before went too smoothly. So smoothly, she thought they were too good to be true.

Maintaining her composure, the Factory Gal turns the live streaming camera in another direction. Today, what she's selling is dreamland, and in a universe that does not dream, dreamland is valuable.

"Three hundred thirty-nine normal, one off-course. The impact point is already stable. Primary rocket engine impact point stable."

"Three hundred thirty-seven enter the scheduled orbit. Two fail to enter . . . "

What happens in the next stretch of time is boring.

The Factory Gal immediately cuts the live stream over to the mechanical octopuses just outside. They rush into the launch site and begin to dismantle and clear the site. Video of this is much more appealing than video of the rockets, which are already turning into tiny points of light.

To go from Earth to Venus, it takes three months.

Those puppets can last on the surface of Venus for one month.

The algae that will scatter from the protective shell, it'll be three months before anyone can confirm that they have survived dormancy. It'll be two hundred forty-three days before anyone knows whether they can grow normally in the endless days and nights of Venus. If they can actually survive, then according to the Shepherd's calculations, after several hundred years, they will effect a change to the air temperature of Venus. The more complex life-forms everyone wants to come into being may take tens of millions of years, even hundreds of millions.

The Factory Gal counts on her fingers.

"In my lifetime, I may see . . . even more algae? This universe really does not dream."

The General glances at her. To speak about what's left of her life in front of an old man, this doesn't seem appropriate. She has just realized this.

But the one who speaks up is the "Spider."

"I'm not even going to see them arrive," he says. "My kernel will be upgraded next month."

The observatory is quiet for a moment. There's only the intermittent buzzing of their instruments.

The General looks stern. With effort, he stands with his cane.

"What's the problem? If we can't see it, we can't see it." He picks up a liquor bottle and takes a few swigs. "The United States launched the first interstellar space probe, called Voyager 1. It will be forty thousand years before it is closer to Gliese 445 than to the Sun. The scientists who launched it never had any hope of seeing that day.

"Forty thousand years is too far. Let's talk about a closer time—those who spent the best years of their lives fighting Nazi Germany, who among them could have seen one hundred fifty years into the future?

"Some things, until you've experienced them, you won't understand. You don't do something just so that you can see how it comes out.

"The universe doesn't dream. The stars in the sky don't dream. As far as the universe is concerned, a human lifetime is incredibly short, but you keep on living. You're willing to fight for even the smallest possibility of getting the result you want. This is enough."

The "Spider" smiles. The face that does not have a face lets out a laugh. A pale plastic hand raises a glass.

"Let's toast to possibilities," he says. "A toast to the universe that does not dream."

They all raise their glasses. Starlight ripples through each glass.

"To possibilities!"

In the Gobi Desert, the launch site has already been cleared away. Mechanical octopuses drag dismantled gear back to the trucks.

A jerboa emerges cautiously and looks around. It picks up a piece of sausage the General dropped then returns to its cave.

The night sky is bright and clear. It has stars, some falling, and many, many rising.

9. Scatter

The Shepherd stays behind. She says Lenghu's geology and climate is highly suitable for breeding plants for Mars. She lives in the observatory, takes care of the General, and breeds her own algae and lichen. Occasionally, she takes a look at Venus through a pair of binoculars. The many tons of algae haven't changed the atmosphere of that planet one bit, but she still keeps looking.

The General falls asleep after a drinking session and never wakes again. In accordance with his will, the Shepherd buries him in the Gobi Desert with a bottle of liquor. The tombstone faces north.

After nineteen upgrades, the Mars project the Spider has been waiting for finally restarts. By then, he no longer remembers that he was once in Lenghu to see off three hundred forty tiny specks in the sky. In the execution phase of the Mars project, though, he still brings a batch of algae. It comes from the Lenghu experimental base. It is the descendent of the descendent of the descendent of the algae the Shepherd bred. The woman who bred the algae is no more, but others have taken over and continue the experiment.

After the Factory Gal leaves Lenghu, she goes to reclaim the discarded rocket engines and failed rockets. She keeps the pointed oval outer shells as a memento. This formally completes the entrustment contract. She spends her life traveling the world, bringing her factory wherever she goes. Sometimes, she happens across some country's abandoned space program. Its data, graphs, blueprints, and even spacecrafts are transported to Lenghu. The Shepherd builds next to the General's tomb a museum of space flight. It holds the artifacts the Factory Gal deposits.

The Factory Gal herself never returns to Lenghu. Traveling to Tonga for a contract, she and her factory are lost in a storm over the Pacific.

The Legs Guy returns to New York. He continues to take care of babies. Many years later, he establishes his own family nurturing camp. Here, young people trying to become parents learn how to take care of infants born from an artificial womb. When he is forty, he marries a woman who came to the camp to study. Over the course of their lives, they have seven children, all fostered by artificial wombs.

10. The Long Tail

After a journey of three long months, the capsules of a grand total of three hundred twenty-six rockets reached their scheduled orbits.

A scorching cloud layer is broken apart by fierce winds into a long river of yellows and browns, flowing quickly over the planet's surface. One after another, the capsules open their doors. Thousands and thousands of gray "date seeds" are inside. The "date seeds" stir up tiny eddies on the smooth cloud layer. In an instant, they are smoothed out by the air current.

Due to atmospheric friction and increase in speed, the "date seeds'" outer shells increase in temperature. They begin to expand due to a special property of their shape-memory alloy. They disintegrate. Wild winds sweep the outer shells of the "date seeds" in all directions. Fragments of gold-colored crystals are swept into Venus' upper atmosphere.

Wrapped in airbags, the avatar puppets slowly drop to the extremely hot surface of Venus. The airbags gradually deflate. The puppets crawl out, filled with anticipation. They begin to receive signals from the orbiting capsules. Meanwhile, they transmit the scenery before their eyes.

Silvery mountains covered by aluminum crystals. Gray lakes of lead. A sky like a fiery forge. Snowflakes fall. These snowflakes are made of crystals of lead sulfate. They are produced on the ground and swept up into the clouds only to fall again.

Via the avatar puppets, players delight in the beautiful scenery before their eyes. At the same time, they start to send a round of actions.

A small hamlet is constructed.

Followed by a catapult.

Players divide themselves into several factions. They attack each other. That never gets boring for them.

One month of effective running time is practically nothing. Before the game server is shutdown, the players have a giant carnival. Tiny puppets ring the hamlet in a happy dance. Then they rush into enthusiastic hugs. In a pile, they sing an out-of-tune song.

At the end of the countdown, via the satellite, players invoke the puppets' self-destruct command.

The explosions on the surface of Venus cause a mushroom cloud to plume. It also leaves a hole, clear evidence of human activity.

Four years later, this hole is filled with lead snow. It disappears without a trace.

In the metaverse, a simulated Venus comes into being. The game continues. The hole lasts far longer there than it does in reality.

The algae that were first thrown into the Venus environment are all dead. The moss also failed to escape that fate. The tiny wind tunnels were not a good simulation of the Venus environment. Not to mention, a bunch of inexpert dreamers did this work. After a few years of not detecting any sign of the algae, virtually everyone who knows about the launch stop following up on it. But after several hundred years, a kind of gas begins to increase steadily in concentration in the upper atmosphere of Venus. It's not the oxygen people hoped for. Instead, it's ammonia in trace amounts.

Some kind of fungus has survived.

This fungus wasn't part of the Shepherd's plan. She put it into the "Venus cocktail" only because it supplied some rare chemical compounds for the algae. But, in the end, it has become the only survivor.

In the violent Venus upper atmosphere, it catches the hot sunlight and flutters randomly in the wind. Gradually, it spreads to the entire atmosphere.

As the fungi increase in density, they begin to come in contact with each other. Old genes that came from the Earth wake again as they mutate. The fungi begin to stick to each other in the atmosphere of Venus. They take the form of a complex cloud organism, swallowing energy, blocking out the sun.

When the "Long Journeys Era" arrives, humanity begins to build a Dyson sphere around the Sun's equator to provide deep spacecrafts a rush of energy. This one act inadvertently reduces the amount of sunlight Venus receives. As a result, the temperature of Venus' atmosphere drops.

In that age, what humanity needs is not a planet, but energy itself. Venus is beneath the notice of most people. Occasionally, a few curious people go to Venus to observe its life-forms. But the universe is too small and the metaverse is too large. They quickly lose interest.

Many thousands of years after the end of the "Long Journeys Era," in the shadow of the broken-down Dyson sphere, the first cloud fish finally fall with the torrential rain to the surface of Venus.

Three hundred million years pass.

The intelligent life of Venus finally takes its first step. They reach the remains of the ancient Dyson sphere, examining the gigantic structure and mysterious remnants that humanity left behind. They guess at what ultimately happened to the ancient civilization that preceded them. But, in the end, they can't find an answer.

On Earth, continents that once were split apart have joined together again. There is a vast, empty central desert. The tiny bit of land once known as Lenghu is still dry and desolate. There's not even one trace of its past. Explorers from Venus flit in the dust and sand, completely oblivious to the fact that this place is where it all started.

After ages of searching, at last, they hear the call from the depths of the Milky Way. It comes from humanity or maybe it comes from some other species.

The stars don't dream.

But civilizations in the universe are just beginning to awake.

Originally published in
Chinese in *A Collection of the 5th Lenghu Award Winning Stories,* 2022.

Translated and published in partnership with Storycom.

ABOUT THE AUTHOR

Chi Hui is a science fiction writer born in the northeast of China, now living in the Southwest with her cat. She began to write in 1993, published her first story in 2003, and is still writing now. She loves food, games, painting, and nature observation. Her science fiction novels include *Terminal Town* and *Artificials 2075*. She also works as an editor at *Science Fiction World*.

Just Another Cat in a Box

E.N. AUSLENDER

The call emerged from the deep of the system's register. Electrical current flowed through the system, returning to the point of the last dimensional fold a nanosecond before the previous activation. A light burned dimly past its expiry in the darkened lab, illuminating shadows on the sole occupant being pulled from his temporal fold and into the present reality within the confines of the matter synthesizer.

Its creator called it a "metal coffin for resurrection." But what did he know? He was dead.

The system's register completed the task. Steam poured from the matter synthesizer's hatch when it opened. The man inside, naked as the moment *He* had been pushed into the temporal fold, inhaled his first breath in millions of years. It smelled of unwashed feet.

The sole lightbulb's gasping illumination pricked his eyes. *He* awoke with annoyance and cursed within the confines of his temporally adrift mind. The thought had traveled from minutes in the future to the present or existed as a persistent stalwart from the start of the laws of physics. *He* couldn't tell. It was all topsy-turvy when one existed outside time, and all thoughts and experiences originated both before and after they happened. Though the only experience within the temporal fold consisted of being pulled apart and reconstructed every single moment of his existence, atom by atom; that, and teaching his temporally suspended mind to whistle.

"*When*" was immaterial. "*Which*" was everything.

Which version had that thought?

He emerged from the metal coffin. The ground was sticky, dim, slightly moist, like someone had spent days licking every square inch of the floor in search of a lost crumb.

Which transit point was this?

The dying light prevented him from seeing the contours of the lab. There was barely enough flowing power in it to poach an atemporal egg. *He* had been promised food and water upon awakening. The temporal fold was a foodless, waterless place, and though *He* neither felt hunger nor thirst within it, he had the awareness that he hadn't eaten in millions of years. Perhaps he might have found that crumb if he began licking the floor.

Which version am I?

Lingering disparate memories from separate versions hung in the prickling darkness like taunting flies nibbling at his skin. The reintegration process should have occurred before *He* awoke. *He* should have remembered the first resurrection from the temporal fold and all subsequent resurrections, regardless of how many there were before the one standing stark nude on the sticky floor. *Perhaps*, *He* thought, *it was like a crowd attempting to run through a single door, but they're all stuck behind one particularly obese person unable to fit through a standard doorframe. I'm sure the system will adjust the doorframe so the particularly obese person can waddle or roll through.*

When no memory threatened to flatten him under its weight, *He* worked through the lab by memory toward where he believed the exit was. Much of this involved shuffling his feet along the sticky floor and holding his hands out in front of him to paw at the vague shadows his eyes could discern. *I must look very silly, He* thought. *This is probably a version test. I was warned about this. Too many prior versions might cause atemporal dysplasia in the brain and turn me into a blubbering cooked ham. They must want to test that my cognitive capabilities are up to snuff.*

Much to his relief, his outstretched hand felt the door handle, and *He* turned it in the way a blubbering cooked ham could not.

Fortunately for him, the door was the exit to the lab. Unfortunately for him, it was the entrance to the stairwell. Given the lab was located in a sub-basement half a kilometer underground to shield the lab's energy reactor or, rather, shield the rest of the world (and the lab) from the energy reactor's radiation, the discovery of the stairwell was unsurprising, albeit disappointing. There was another door somewhere in the lab that led to the elevator, and *He* gave returning to the darkness of the lab a serious thought. It was an incredibly serious thought, actually, and *He* pulled the lab door open only to be inundated by the stench of thousands of unwashed feet. Somehow the smell had been amplified in the brief moment he'd left the lab, as if a horde of temporally displaced teenagers had appeared in the lab after their gym class and left their socks behind.

He closed the door and ascended one step at a time.

Despite being in the peak condition *He* had been in the moment he had been sent into the atemporal fold, his ascent up the stairs could not be done atemporally. His legs wobbled and decided they'd rather take a nap than continue up the seemingly endless stairs.

This is probably also . . . a physical test. To test . . . my endurance.

He never believed his internal monologue could be out of breath until that moment. After resorting to ascending the stairs on his hands and feet like an oversized hairy frog, he made it to the very top exit moist as a regular frog. Sweat layers between his hands and the floor caused him to slip while he crawled out from the exit into the main building.

Natural light flooded in through high windows in the empty, dusty entrance hall. What had once been the world's grandest scientific research center was a hollow cavern of forgotten brilliance. Red dust littered the ground. Wind blustered through the hollow windows.

"Hel, hello?" *He* called out. "I require cortical reintegration."

His voice echoed back at him. *He* pushed himself up from the floor, only to find his lower body stained red with dust. Looking down, *He* found himself reminded of the nose of a very silly-looking monkey. *What was it called? Probably Monkey? No . . . Problematic Monkey? Proboscis Monkey. That's it. The asynchronous memory is interfering with my thought recall. What strange dust.*

Portions of the dust on the floor were unevenly coated. Upon closer inspection, the uneven coatings were due to footprints that had not been made that long ago. *He* followed the footprints to a table in the middle of the atrium. On the table was a single old-style monitor and a spare micro-generator plugged into it, along with a curious thing *He* thought he'd never see again.

Just in front of the screen was a black leather notebook with *paper* inside. Paper! Where in the world would anyone get the spare trees for it? There hadn't been any spare trees on the planet since the Arboreal Wars Treatise.

On the notebook's cover was a pink piece of paper with numerous scribbles inscribed, all in the same handwriting.

"Important," *He* read aloud, "watch curated logs of Versions: 11,023, 27,277, 73,256, 890,193, unknown. Then open notebook."

What a strange order of events, He thought. He placed his thumb under the cover and almost opened it, but then sense got the better of him, and he tapped the monitor. This was clearly how every other version did it, so *He* had to do the same. The logs were already queued in the correct order.

"Version 11,023, log ten," said the previous version of him, wearing a strange silver suit with an inelastic hood. "The war finally ended yesterday."

"*War*?"

"We've been attempting to reconstruct the power transits, but we have no idea if the other centers are doing the same, or even if anyone is still there. Both the M'vinka and the Grimchak Calordian failed in obtaining our reactors before they buggered off, but there's no telling if they'd succeeded with the others."

"Which in the hell are those?"

"According to Professor [a low guttural sound superseded by two high tones], the damage done to the planet's biosphere is cumulative. It believes there's a way to sort out all this mess, but only time will tell. It will start rebuilding the sensor net to give us an idea of what we're dealing with. Version 11,023, signing off."

He looked around the cavernous entrance hall. It hummed with the wind spilling in through the broken windows. He accessed the next log.

"Version 27,277, log twenty-nine," the new version said, wearing a black matte mask that muffled his voice. "Professor [a low guttural sound superseded by two high tones] managed to finish the sensor net, finally, but it's not good news. As we feared, the planet's biosphere has been almost completely wiped out. The atmosphere is quickly turning toxic. Professor [a low guttural sound superseded by two high tones] and I can survive the degradation, but there is nothing we can do for all the inhabitants of this planet. Zvestaya died." His voice broke, and he looked away, though it was impossible to tell with the dark mask where he was looking or what he was feeling. "Professor [a low guttural sound superseded by two high tones] helped me adjust future versions for increased atmospheric endurance as the environment continues degrading. We'll try to work through the problem. Zvestaya would have . . . " He quieted again. "We have not yet detected other centers, but that may be due to the increased dust storms. We will keep trying. Version 27,277, signing off."

The entrance hall felt emptier than it had been, as if the ghosts of all the long dead still haunted the place. *He* accessed the next log.

"Version 73,256, log forty." The version was as plain and naked as *He* was at that moment, but there was stress in his skin. "Professor [a low guttural sound superseded by two high tones] has died. It believed inserting itself as a backup power generator for the sensor net would expand its detection gradient. The sad thing was, it was correct, at least for the ten seconds it boosted its resolution. But we detected something emitting chroniton radiation and abnormal concentrations of tachyons. It was detected just long enough for us to get a location on the southern continent nine thousand kilometers away. But our power is failing. I had to fish out a notebook from storage to write down the coordinates. *Paper*. Weird, isn't it? It's been thousands of years since anyone wrote on paper. But our power systems are failing. The reactor's developed a stress fracture, and there's no one to fix it, except me. I've dialed back all the facility usage to lower its output, but the crack is expanding. I'm going to try to fix it. And so will you."

The log clicked off. *He* touched the notebook. No memory leeched from it into his skin. It remained a quiet object, worn down on its cover, though not as much as he might have expected given the version differential listed between the previous log and the next one. *He* started the log.

"Version 890,193, log . . . I don't remember," the new version said. Red dust had filled in visible burns and scarring on his face. Each breath was labored. "I've been unable to repair the reactor. It exploded and destroyed the only path off the mountain. Well, not a mountain anymore. Plateau. It's been too many years. Too many years . . . " The version breathed hard, gulping as if he were a fish on land. "Power is left to just batteries. I've lowered the draw capacity of the atemporal recall and completely cut off the reintegration protocols. I'll have to find a spare power source for the computer . . . I'd hoped to get a message to that location . . . I've had time to calculate the potential of what we detected. Had to do it by hand to save power. The amount of energy it gives off, it has to be a temporal displacement device. If it is, our directive is to reach the displacement device. This is mandate above all else. We must use it to go back and prevent the conflict from ever happening."

"That's not possible," *He* said.

"You're going to say, 'that's not possible,' because you haven't had the time to process the information like we have," the version said. "But it is."

"You're just delusional from—"

"And I'm not delusional," the version said, and *He* shut up. "Remember, you won't have reintegrated memories. You won't know what I know. You have to trust me. I'll develop a plan to get off this plateau. I just . . . "

The version collapsed off-screen, and the log ended. Only one log remained: *unknown*. Unknown version. *He* didn't know if he should trust an unknown version. All the versions were supposed to be numbered, after all. It was a bit like trusting a man with no name to handle your finances, only to find that the man had utilized his anonymity to completely change his identity to yours and subsequently steal your wife, children, and thirteen-year-old labradoodle because, in this nightmarish scenario, he's just another version of you but with slightly different proclivities. After all, if he had something by which he identified himself, he certainly wouldn't be you.

He looked around, half-hoping someone would jump out from behind a counter to tell him this was all an elaborate hoax. The thought of an overly complex conspiratorial scenario to scare him was almost preferable to reality. *He* tapped the last log entry.

A version very much like him appeared. Red dust stained his face and chest and caked his hair into small burgundy mountains. There was a wild look about him, as if epiphany had crept up behind him and forcibly wiggled into his backside.

"If this log is being viewed," the unknown version said with red dust falling off his upper lip, "then bite your tongue and listen." *He* felt the need to retort to himself, but the version continued. "I know how to get off the plateau. First, pause this log and go outside. Don't ask any questions or get snooty or think about how much your penis looks like the nose of a proboscis monkey. They don't exist anymore, it's very sad, I shed my tears already. Go out the front door. If there's a sandstorm, wait until it's over."

He glanced toward the entrance. Where there had been glass doors emblazoned with the acronym of the Centre under the Mountain with a Nuclear Gunderson-Reactor was instead a red vista of hazy cloud and spinning dust plinking off the atrium's pylons.

"Well don't just look at it," the version said. *He* rolled his eyes and paused the log. The red dust on the floor grew thicker as *He* walked across the atrium toward the entrance. Dust started tickling his toenails ten meters away from the entrance, and when *He* looked down, *He* saw imprints of previous footsteps mostly erased by the continuing wind. *He* gulped, feeling the dust scratch his throat, and continued outside.

Visibility was negligible in the constant wind. *He* staggered out a bit further, a meter away from the entrance, two, covering his eyes to peer through the flinging dust.

This is intolerable. Which am I supposed to see?

The sky shone in patches of blue amid the torrent of dirt and dust flung about, though it was the sort of blue one's tongue gets after ingesting too many blue candies and vomiting all over their parents' new coffee table. *He* nearly turned to go back inside when the dust storm broke for a moment.

Before him was a cliff that led to a canyon. *No, He* thought to himself as he walked forward, *not a canyon.*

A canyon might have been shaped by ancient rivers and unnerving winds, winding and wearing down old mountains into plateaus and jagged edges into smoothed curves. What lay before him was a crater as old as a canyon and wider and deeper than an ocean. The cliff on which *He* stood was one of few that had survived around the impact point, but otherwise all *He* saw was the several million-year-old remnants of a massive explosion.

There used to be a road leading straight out of the center's entrance to the small city just thirty minutes' walk away. Tree coverage along the road was so dense that rainy days would sound like roaring ocean waves. The road led to the middle of town, an amphitheater, where every night a play or a concert or a gathering would enrapture the town's residents. Now, dust tornadoes sprung up in the distance, littering the crater ground. They might have been kilometers wide, but to him, they could fit in the palm of his hand.

He returned inside and continued the log.

"Yes, I know. As best I can figure based on the accumulated logs, and I've gone through all of them, literally, and curated the important ones so you don't have to slog through them all and suffer a minor existential crisis. You're very welcome, by the way," the version said. He cleared his throat. "The crater was the result of the war mentioned by some of our earliest versions. Unfortunately, the dust storms brought on by ecological collapse have sped up the mountain's weathering and CUMWANGR's defense grid couldn't be expanded around it to prevent the mountain eroding. Coupled with the reactor exploding, well, it's been a very angering day. We've been left alone for quite a while. I can't be certain since I don't know what version I am, but it's been at least three million years since our first version was activated. Probably. Anyway, that's not important."

"Not important? How is that not important?" *He* shouted.

"Will you shut up and listen to me?" the version snapped. "There's a bigger problem. I've estimated the distance between the crater floor and the cliff's edge to be approximately seven thousand meters, accounting for the approximately twenty-five-degree gradient curve at the bottom. And . . . there's nothing in the center we can use to lower down safely. We're stuck, except . . . " He heaved a breath. "Except if we build a staircase."

He felt the color drain from his face immediately.

"No . . . "

"Yes," the version said. "I've estimated—"

"That would be absurd!"

"—given descent and landing angle, as well as our body width—"

"No, no, no . . . "

"—it would take approximately four hundred thousand of us to create a hill of sufficient height and width to allow one of us to leave the center and search for the temporal displacement device."

He sprinted to the entrance. Wind whipped at his face, and *He* slipped on the dust, but he righted himself and pushed through the cloud. The cliff's edge was invisible through the storm. *He* knelt onto his hands and knees and crawled forward until he felt the edge and poked his head below the level to see what number *He* he was.

Spots of the dust storm cleared for him to see, approximately thirty meters below, the form of a man. Clarity increased. Caked in red dust, hundreds of thousands of versions beneath him became visible as a large clump of red mountain, with the one lying on top only slightly more visible than the others due to what was likely the impact of the previous version landing on him and wiping some of the dust off.

He pulled back from the edge.

In that moment, it wasn't hard to imagine how many times the same scenario had played out. A previous version wakes up and is confused by the darkness, climbs the stairs, watches the logs, questions and doubts the logs' content because of the lack of memory integration, discovers the bodies, has a minor meltdown, and then eventually jumps out of a sense of obligation. *Obligation? No, not obligation. Duty? No. Necessity? No. Inevitability? Which one is it?*

He trudged back into the atrium and rewound the log to where he'd left it.

"—search for the temporal displacement device." The version went quiet, probably realizing what the watcher would do. *He* remained quiet as well. His eyes drifted down to his hands and feet. They were caked in dust, and in the reflection of the quiet screen, his hair was, too. *He* matched the version he saw.

"Yes, I know," the version finally said. "This is a real death. We were told this wouldn't happen, and yet, here we are. There will be no benefit from past experience, though I believe this to be the real benefit. Those who jump the earliest will have to watch the ground approach them. Those who jump as the hill gets closer to the cliff's edge won't die as quickly. They may even survive for a time. Broken bones, severed spines, you name it, it'll happen. But we need to get the hill as high as possible as quickly as possible so one of us can leave this . . . tomb before power runs out. As long as the light in the lab is on, we've still got some hope. For you who has discovered the leap is manageable, I have written out approximate directions to the known location of the temporal displacement device in the notebook. You must be certain the leap is survivable before taking the notebook, though. A broken leg will kill you long before you reach the device. I believe, based on predicted stability of the pile of bodies and our bone density, as well as visibility issues from the dust storms and the granularity of the dust, we could potentially survive a leap of five meters in poor conditions without disability. Feel free to double-check my calculations. They're in the notebook. For everyone else . . . you know what you have to do."

The version stopped speaking and stared into the camera.

"What if the lightbulb is almost dead?" *He* said.

"No, you don't just swan dive, you idiot. Don't be sarcastic. Try to angle your descent so the wind pushes you toward the cliff face, but not so you roll against it," the version replied. "I believe an angle of impact—"

"What if the lightbulb is almost dead?" his voice rose.

"—of around seventy-three degrees relative to the upward curve should be enough to—"

"The lightbulb is almost dead! What do I do if the lightbulb is almost dead? You said as long as the light is still on there is hope, but damn it, the light is almost dead! What do I do?"

"—land at the base of the cliff without rolling far. This way, at least, we can eliminate some of the unhelpfulness caused by some of us landing in a useless spot."

"Wait, wait," *He* said to the version as if he could reply, and exited the log screen. "I can query the system to see how long it's been on, it's not a problem. That can tell me how long the light's been on and how long it has left."

The system's power notary read as 2.0866486e+10. The value was delineated in collected hours. Given the computer's relative simplicity and low energy usage, it was unable to translate the term into years. It took *He* only a moment to realize how long the computer had been operating.

"Two-point-four million . . . " *He*'s legs wobbled, and he fell bum-first onto the dusty floor. The calculations of how many had jumped with the time difference from the last counted log led to only one conclusion: there had been many who had jumped and survived far too long with traumatic injuries. With *He's* advanced physiology, it was possible to live for a thousand years. If severely injured, it might measure in the dozens or hundreds. And because they had all decided to follow the directive to build the staircase, they never moved. They'd lain on the mountain broken and collected dust for decades, centuries, waiting to die so the next version could be awoken.

The last operating schematic for the center's batteries showed an estimated life span of one million years at standard operation. Calculating for low power operation extended it to two, but *He* didn't know how much energy the matter synthesizer needed for each recall, nor what drip of power was needed for the lightbulb, and it was impossible to tell because every system in the center besides the log computer was offline. Either way, the intersection of just enough power and no more was far closer than *He* was comfortable with. *Could I risk energy running out mid-recall for a new version?*

He returned to the unknown log and continued playing it.

"The only problem with that is," the version said, "there aren't any curtains left. Trust me, I've checked. No, I'm not obsequious to the interior designer. In case you haven't noticed, there are no interior designers on the planet nor anyone else to design anything. So no, we cannot make a parachute out of the storage curtains because there aren't any." The version went silent. *He* stared at the log. "Look, I'm not going to talk with you if you're going to warble inanities like that. You know what your duty is, so do it. This was always our directive: be humanity's soldier. If we don't do it now, there's no humanity. Now do it."

The log turned off. *He* opened it again.

"Now do it."

Again.

"Now do it."

"You idiot," *He* said, and shut off the log. Red winds howled through the broken windows. *He* heaved a sigh and slammed his head against the notebook in front of the computer. Red dust coughed out from the pages. "Ow."

Which option do I choose?

He lifted his head off the notebook. The pink note had been crinkled. He opened the notebook cover.

IF THE STAIRCASE ISN'T HIGH ENOUGH YET, DON'T READ FURTHER. JUMP YOU IDIOT, the first page said. *He* turned the page.

YOU'D BETTER NOT BE READING THIS IF THE STAIRCASE ISN'T HIGH ENOUGH YET.

Next page.

TRY TO LAND ON YOUR STOMACH, NOT YOUR FEET.

Next page.

HOW MANY TIMES DO I HAVE TO TELL YOU, JUMP!

The next pages contained the coordinates for the temporal displacement device along with calculations of its power output. *He* kept flipping until he found writing that looked more recent than the rest. It was the last bit of writing in the notebook.

If you're reading this, then you're probably in the same pickle I was. Batteries look low. Staircase height is just out of reach. I guess there were some things we couldn't predict. I wish I had a weapon of some kind to shoot myself in the head so you could use me to break your fall. Seems like that would have been easier, wouldn't it? I thought about breaking my own neck, but I couldn't bring myself to do it since I'd live too long. If I'm the last, and I end the line by breaking my own neck instead of landing on the staircase, I've killed myself thinking I did something right by ignoring the directive. Then again, who in the hell is going to judge me, my red powdered penis?

The light still seemed to have a bit of juice. I chose to check it before I wrote this. My legs are burning. Goddamn stairs. I also checked around the lab for curtains. No luck.

I hope someone reads this. I suppose that's why I'm going to jump. It's not what we signed up for, but who am I to disagree with myself? It's a bit sad, though—it would have been nice to remember our name. I guess what happens next is entirely up to you.

He stared at the last line until its imprint lingered in his eyes. The atrium was suddenly very hollow.

There was both a decision to make and none at all. It was actually quite a bit like existing in an atemporal fold, though the irony wasn't immediately apparent to him. *He* closed the notebook and straightened out the pink note on the cover. What memories were available to him from the days before the process were happy, though every memory before this day was emboldened by the insanity of it.

He could at least be satisfied knowing those memories would be available to the next version. Because there had to be a next version.

The blustering winds howled a greeting to him, and he walked out of the atrium to the cliff. For a moment, the clouds and dust parted, and far on the horizon was a sun ensconced in red, shimmering like a ruby dangling from a spiderweb. The wind was nothing more than the clattering of the rain on the old trees, like waves crashing on the shore.

He jumped stomach-first. Numerous bones broke and punctured several organs. *He* closed his eyes and waited to discover which injury would kill him first.

Sometime later, the lightbulb flickered.

ABOUT THE AUTHOR

E.N. Auslender has written a few stories. Some of them are considered pretty decent for being written by a marmoset. That's not to say that E.N. Auslender is a marmoset afraid of admitting he's a marmoset and being shunned by both humans and the marmoset community, but he isn't saying that, either. His stories aren't about marmosets. Mostly.

Rail Meat

MARIE VIBBERT

It wasn't a glamorous entrée into the world of the rich. Ernestine jimmied a service door and climbed forty flights of dingy, bare metal stairs to avoid the sensors in the hotel elevators. Maids and mechanics locked eyes, disapprovingly, then decided she wasn't their problem and slid past her with professional unseeing.

At the top floor, she paused, getting her breathing under control as she hastily wiped the sweat from her forehead and opened the pleats on her smartFit, converting it instantly from a bodysuit to a cocktail dress. With a stomp, heels popped out of her convertible shoes. Then she took down her bun and fluffed her hair. This was her armor, and out there was the battle. Head high, she burst forth into cool evening breezes, tropical smells, and the murmur of voices over cocktails being stirred. Overhead, atmosphere-skimming yachts blazed lines of fire that must have been walls of inferno close-up but looked like tiny scratches in the curving ceiling of twilight. Ernestine turned her gaze lower, on the pockets and wrists and tables where the very rich casually placed the very expensive.

First, she liberated a gin and tonic, half-drunk with lipstick on the rim. Holding a drink made you less suspicious.

Her first opportunity was very nice—a ruby ring, of all things, left on a side table. She palmed it fast, but her nail polish turned from blue to red. Damn, tracking chip. She returned the ring to its spot unobtrusively and crossed the party. There were bound to be dropped items by the band.

A slender wrist hung casually over the edge of the roof railing, wearing a data bracelet big enough to slip off. The young man faced the band, oblivious. Ernestine took hold of the bracelet only to have that wrist turn and the hand attached to it grasp her own. Deep, dark eyes grabbed her attention just as surely. "It's a knockoff, sweetheart, you won't get as much as I paid for the games on it."

Fuck. She tried for a casual smile, "Oh, I was just checking the make . . . I'm a dealer in—" His smirk deepened, and he tilted his head as if to say, "Yes, please continue to try and scam me while I scramble your brains with my beauty."

Ernestine dropped the act. "How did you get past the body scanners?" If he was a con artist like her, he might have a new hack to share, and he didn't look like he climbed forty flights. He looked like he'd never sweated in his life.

He leaned with boneless grace, like a cat against the parapet. He picked up an unattended martini with only a swallow left and frowned at it. "Delivered a pizza to the fifteenth floor. They have those, here—human food delivery."

"Swank." She gestured at his data bracelet. "No hard feelings, between professionals?"

He grinned like she'd complimented him, shrugging amiably, and Ernestine felt a dangerous swoop in her heart. It wasn't easy, finding a lover that understood the thieving life.

But that wasn't why she was here. She peeled her eyes away from him. "I'll work the eastern side of the roof. We won't get in each other's way."

"You're wasting your time. The real money is up there." He flicked his deep-set eyes upward, where the yacht races painted traces against the twilight, like shooting stars.

"No one's leaving valuables lying around on a racing yacht."

"You think too small." The fire from the skies danced across his feral grin.

So, he had a big score in mind. Interesting. She could slide along beside him and sweep it from his grasp. She leaned on the railing next to him, angled so they were together, watching the crowd. "Ernestine."

"Rico."

The twist of his lips told her it wasn't his real name. Well, neither was hers. "What's the prize, then, the rich person's yacht?"

"The rich person." His mouth hung open like he could already taste his victory. He drained the swallow of martini and tossed the drink glass off the roof.

She waited to hear the crash of glass. It never came. She peered over the rail. Ten stories below, an energy field sparkled, the glass bobbing like a stone in water toward a slot in the building side. Did he know there was a debris-catching field when he did that? He was smirking at her when she straightened. Irritating. And a bored rich woman was no prize she could scoop up on the side. "Right. You already have the attitude, but no one's taking applications for trophy husband."

"I don't wait for invitations. Tomorrow, I'm going up there."

Getting onto a racing yacht would take more than a scanner-jammer or a man-in-the-middle attack on a pizza joint. How would he even get up to the launching station? "Impossible."

"Only improbable. I signed on as rail meat." He smoothed a hand down his chest, pressing already-tight fabric against muscle.

Meat, indeed. She shook her head to clear the lust-fog. "Excuse me, Rail *what*?"

"Rail meat. For the races." He looked at her like this jargon was as commonplace as "martini." "You volunteer to act as living ballast."

Human ballast? "That sounds needlessly evil. Don't they have, I don't know, machines?"

"It's tradition. Since the days of water races."

"Good god, that sounds dangerous."

His smile was violent. "It is. Running across a slick deck, no safety lines, and if you fall overboard the survival rate is abysmal."

"Why would anyone do that?"

He took a lazy step back, and another. She felt the empty space pulling her toward him. His smile turned wistful. "To catch an open heart."

Oh no. If someone had dropped a money chip or even a diamond right then, she wouldn't have gone for it. There was no prize on this terrace more worth stealing than this fascinating young man.

Rico's designated target was one Kelly Cher Knight, heiress to a gig assigning empire. Millions of people hustling for pennies paid for her sleek stratosphere yacht, and her sleek upswept hairdo that matched it. Rico showed Ernestine her picture, pulling it out on a projected display over his knockoff data bracelet as they lay together in sweat-soaked sheets in his downtown apartment.

"She looks like a really ugly fashion model."

Rico snorted. "She's one of the better ones, and single. I've been combing her socials for all her likes and dislikes, back five years. I dyed my hair black for her and removed my tattoos."

Ernestine pulled his wrist and its projection down to the mattress and straddled his waist. "That's insane. You haven't even met this person."

He playfully tried to buck her off. "*Yet*. I have an in. My cousin has a coworker who was rail meat last year, on her ship."

"Hrmm." Ernestine trapped both his wrists and leaned down. She'd been doing her homework between the first and second date. "From what

I've read, most of the rail meat are friends-of-friends, poor relations, that kind of thing. People who already have a foot in the door. They are not welcoming to the poor and pretty who want to take their place."

Rico stretched, pressing against her hold, reveling in it more than trying to break free. "No, but this fellow caught the flu, and took two others out with him."

"How *convenient*." She meant it flirtatiously, but real suspicion slipped into her tone, cooling the mood.

He rolled her off of him. "Not *that* convenient."

Ernestine considered how she'd get a hold of, say, the pillowcase of someone suffering through the flu and leave it in another person's clean laundry. She shook her head. "I still say stealing is the better way to go. It's a sure thing. Money and jewels don't change their mind when they see a younger thief more willing to go down on them."

"Well, I am expecting to find lots of money and jewels lying around a well-sated heiress." He kissed her nose and got up, pulling a towel off the bedpost and wrapping it around his waist. The sun cut through the dusty window and over his sculpted body.

Ernestine wished she had a camera-eye to capture him. "Fair enough. Two others, though? Does that mean there's room for me, too?"

He could have mocked her for changing her tune, but his smile was kind, his shrug expansive, an invitation to everything.

He'd already shown her how generous he could be. The foolish boy might even cover for her if she got caught robbing his intended. She followed him with her eyes until the bathroom door shut. She groaned. It was a risky con, and she'd have to watch him fail at his doomed quest to become a kept man before she got close enough to steal everything Kelly Cher hadn't tied down. That wouldn't be fun.

But she already knew she was going to do it. She could never turn down chasing a pretty, expensive thing.

Ernestine fumbled with the unfamiliar, bulky gloves, checking the seals on her borrowed pressure suit. It felt like wearing someone else's used sneaker, two sizes too big.

Kelly Cher Knight had a perfect doll's nose much too small for the rest of her features, which looked more artificial in person. She also ruined it with a sneering expression, looking over her crew like they were clumps of dirt. Her body, however, was all that money could buy, perfect hemispherical breasts and obvious hip implants displayed in a skintight pressure suit that underscored how bulky the "rail meat" suits were.

Well, Ernestine didn't have to win her heart. She only wanted an invitation to a gala, maybe, some earned time near the very rich and their very portable wealth. That would be gotten by being competent and unexceptional . . . and surviving this.

Kelly Cher tossed her perfect, immobile hair and adjusted the neck-ring on her suit. "Don't worry about the first buoy, we nailed that in simulation with no help, but I'll need everyone hard to port after it. Quint thinks he owns turn two."

"We'll show him," Rico declared with his winning smile, but Kelly Cher reacted to it like a piece of furniture had dared ask her for the time.

She secured her helmet, and her next words came out over the suit radios. "Keep up and watch for my signals. I'm not coming in second because of your inexperienced asses."

Ernestine followed Rico out onto the yacht, stomach in her throat from the sudden, vast drop around them. The ship itself was a splinter of a thing, gently patterned like shark skin, the gleaming silver rails hanging out over the twilight-colored atmosphere. Earth curved alarmingly below.

Ernestine's knees quaked as she grabbed the nearest rail. Rico pulled her away. "Stay on center. There are toeholds."

Half-circle bumps ran along the center line of the deck, which sloped down to each side, like a spinal column poking through the smooth scales of a shark's back. It didn't feel like the most secure hold, shoving her foot under one, but she had Rico holding onto her.

The other ships were farther away than she expected. Her breath was loud in her helmet. "Where's the buoy? I can't see it."

"No one can, only the pilots." Rico jerked his helmet back toward Kelly Cher, who was clipping her safety line (*she* got one) to the deck behind the pilot's wheel.

Overhead, the solar sails curtained down, silently snapping into place. Ernestine knew from the articles she'd read the night before, and from the other ships, that a spar extended down below them as far as the mast was above. They were an absurd, exaggerated balance toy, hanging on nothing.

Far too soon, the platform beneath her jerked to life, and they were off.

At first it was like trying to surf . . . in a surf simulator, the board bucking under her feet, keeping her balance without much effort, but aware she could lose it, then Kelly Cher shouted, "PORT!" and everyone threw themselves left. It was a breathless scamper, hardly three steps, and her hips were hitting the bar. Her hands slipped and slapped at the smooth rail.

Rico caught her, showed her how to hook her arm around the rail to hang on. "Careful! If you fall, they don't catch you."

It was a joke she'd heard a few times that day in the locker room. Each of them had a bulky parachute on their back that would theoretically deploy when they reached a certain altitude, bringing them down safely . . . somewhere on Earth. If they were lucky. The hazards were mostly non-racing aircraft, or being blown into a mountain, or simply landing somewhere so remote no one got to you.

Or you could drop safely down in a city and get hit by a commuter train.

Ernestine did not intend to fall.

"CENTER!" Kelly Cher shouted, and Ernestine discovered that stopping on that tiny toehold was a lot harder than hooking herself on a rail. She missed, slid past, fell, and had to grab on with her hand, struggling to get herself back to center, almost making it when Kelly Cher shouted "PORT" again.

It was like skating on an iceberg that was hurtling through space. What was she doing? This wasn't worth it. She could have stayed on land, stalked the hotel parties. She'd let herself fall blind to the dangers because of a pretty boy who had screwed her brains clean out of her head.

And now said pretty boy was casually muscling his way closer to the pilot's wheel, standing like the ground was solid beneath his feet. "I see what you're doing, taking the southern course. Bold!"

Kelly Cher gazed right through him and hollered, "STARBOARD!"

When Rico hit the rail beside Ernestine, far from discouraged, he was grinning like he could take a bite out of the moon, and it would ask him to do it again. Below them, roiling orange flames broke the twilight colors in a turbulent wave of heat. Color caressed his parted lips, his sculpted cheek, beyond reach behind the curve of his helmet.

Maybe he was worth it.

Ernestine slipped again, and for a breathless moment, she hung over the Earth, only his arms holding her, dragging her back to the rail.

He pressed to her, a comforting wall on one side, his arm a safety belt. "We're halfway. You can make it, Ernestine. Only two more turns, and we're in the final stretch. We're winning!"

They moved to center again, and Ernestine decided she wasn't too proud to crawl. Behind them, Kelly Cher had eyes for nothing but the space ahead, for the buoy signals only she could see. Ernestine clung to Rico's ankle and elbowed him in the thigh. "How is this impressing your lady-love?"

"When she wins, they'll throw a crew party, and she'll stop by after her victory party. That's when I make my move." He helped Ernestine up. "I only need a moment."

"I hate you right now."

He laughed. "I know."

Twice more, he tried to talk to Kelly Cher, heroic efforts of poise and balance between desperate scrambles. Once, he must have told a pretty funny joke because she laughed, but it wasn't a kind laugh.

Were they even winning? Ernestine hadn't seen the other racers. It was hard to find a terror-free moment to look, and then she only saw whatever happened to be directly in front of her, and that tended to be a nausea-inducing slice of darkening atmosphere.

Kelly Cher shouted, "STARBOARD!"

Ernestine made it this time without falling or needing help. Something overhead flared, a flash of light. A falling star? Here? So close they could catch it in their hands?

"FUCKING QUINT!" Kelly Cher screamed.

No one had said how to respond to that command.

Rico reached centerline before Ernestine, pointing up. "Quint took a high arc, he's going to beat us to the final mark. He must have jettisoned his ballast. Gutsy."

Kelly Cher swung her leg around the base of her wheel, stepping half in front of it as she gestured wide with one hand. "I need to lighten this craft a hundred pounds, now! Someone jump."

The rail meat all froze where they are. Rico, Ernestine, and two people she'd only met in the locker room.

Kelly Cher waved frantically with one arm, leaning out like a dog on a chain, like she would push them off herself if she could step away from the wheel. "Cowards! If none of you jump, I'll sue you all!"

"This is it," Rico straightened. "My chance to impress her."

Ernestine read the hesitation in his spine as he stepped forward. She grabbed for him, but he slipped from her grasp as easily as mist.

She could throw herself over. It would be the only way to stop him. She pictured it. She took a step. Rico saluted Kelly Cher. "Look me up on the way down." He stepped onto the rail and fell backward, one hand outstretched toward Kelly Cher like she was his lifeline. It was dramatic and flawless.

And Kelly Cher was already yanking the wheel, shouting orders, her whole sculpted body straining with the craft. "AFT, everyone, AFT and PORT!"

Ernestine tumbled with the others, her shock and rage following after her until she hit the rail, with no comforting presence, no strong arm to support her as the roiling flames seemed to lick hungrily up the side of the boat at her. The craft screamed, some deep pain of metal, and the wind beat her, as solid as wet concrete.

She was furious. Rico would throw his beautiful body, his passion and skill, over a rail for this random woman. And now she was risking her own life for a man she'd just met who wasn't there anymore, a man who chanced death to spend ten minutes at an after-party.

They had better not put that on her tombstone.

Ernestine barely had a coherent thought through the finish line, and then the craft gentled, gliding into dock, the big elevator station arriving so abruptly to fill her vision.

Kelly Cher unhooked her safety line and whooped. She leaped into the huddle of crew, throwing an arm over Ernestine. "We did it! I LOVE You!"

And then she was gone, skipping away into a cacophony of fireworks.

Ernestine did not want to go to the after-party. She wanted to get her feet on solid ground and a shower, in that order, and it was only when she was standing under the spray in the joint locker room for all the yacht crews that she remembered to fumble her own bracelet on and look for Rico's location.

His bracelet, at least, had survived the fall. In fact, its location dot was flashing along the rail line from the coast. Ernestine turned her back to the shower spray and gestured to call him.

The relief buckled her knees when his face appeared, bruised and mussed but somehow more handsome even for that. He was hunched over, the train roof and other passengers in the background. "Worried about me? I'll be at least another two hours. Keep the party going until I get there, Ernie. I'm relying on you!"

You fucker, she thought. Absolutely not. She hung up.

She wasn't going to go to the party. She wasn't. She dried off and got dressed and checked her messages planning on not going to the party. She walked to the train fully intending to hop on the route toward her home.

Then, because she had neither dignity nor self-respect, she got on the one leading to the hotel where the parties were planned. Because he would be there. Damn him. She didn't like him, but she still wanted him.

She couldn't pretend any longer that she was doing this for the pickpocketing. It was an opportunity she'd have killed for a month ago. Hell, a day ago. Her invitation code was picked up from her bracelet at the hotel doors, and they opened without fuss, granting her free access to a space rife with wealth and possessions.

The security around the VIP celebration was as tight as an airlock, but there was an overflow bar in the hallway with a glass wall offering a panorama of the district and tiny cocktail tables. She picked up a few gold coins that had no doubt been left as tips and a glass of champagne from a passing waiter—not previously sipped.

It ought to have improved her mood. It didn't. She stalked the periphery of the parties, perfunctorily looking for easy marks and loose change. Really, she was looking for him, and it galled her. She'd become as stupid as he was.

She made it to the actual crew party for her ship, which included all the maintenance and ground techs, just after Kelly Cher showed up with her big golden cup and fawning entourage. Everyone in the room converged on the trophy, like filaments in the presence of a strong magnet. Ernestine went to the buffet thinking it didn't matter if she were there or not. At least she could fill up on salmon puffs printed to look like the yacht.

She watched Kelly Cher soak up the fawning, looking past the people around her like there was some real audience behind them. Ernestine wanted to seethe, but the puffs were crunchy and fluffy, and the paste inside was spiced with delicate herbs that made her instantly feel she was on the seashore at springtime. Damn, and this was the below-the-salt stuff. She wrapped two more in napkins and tucked them in her pocket.

The congratulations had all been said at least twice, and the enthusiasm was dying down. Kelly Cher sighed dramatically, "Oh, but I have to goooo."

And then the door to the hall burst open and there was Rico, his shirt open to the waist, breathless and glowing with sweat. He spread his arms wide. "How was my dive?"

Kelly Cher actually looked at him. A few of her courtiers stepped back to give her an open view.

Ernestine didn't decide to take four hard strides forward. She didn't decide to raise her arm. It just happened, but when her palm hit his perfect jaw and the slap reverberated oh so magnificently, she was very grateful to her subconscious. This time.

She didn't pause to admire her handiwork, striding out the still-open doors and not stopping until she was on the subway platform.

Ernestine had two slightly crushed salmon puffs for breakfast with bitter coffee and sat down to count her meager spoils on the kitchen counter.

Okay, they weren't meager. A real gold rosary, enough hard coinage to pay the month's rent, and one of those data rings that did half as much as a bracelet but somehow cost more. She spun it on its end and considered she had also had a thrilling experience. Real terror was hard to come by safely, and oh so much better in rearview. She had gotten stories for a lifetime.

Someone knocked on her door.

She stopped the spinning ring with the flat of her hand. "You'd better not," she said to no one but herself, already certain it was him.

It was. She opened the door to a rainbow bouquet of gladiolus and daylilies. Rico peeked around it. "Can I come in?"

"Do those have solid gold stems?"

He lowered the bouquet. "I was touched, that you worried so for me."

"Did that slap say 'worried'? It was supposed to say 'pissed.'"

Ugh. His smile was knowing and fond. "It was perfect. My entrance was good, but it was the slap, I could tell, that won her over. Everyone wants what belongs to someone else."

"Oh." Ernestine felt her stomach drop. She snatched the bouquet from his hand. "When's the wedding?"

He rested his cheek on the door jamb. "I've no idea. And sympathies to the eventual groom. She dismissed me in the morning like a hooker and wouldn't even look at me when I crashed her brunch."

Ernestine shook her head. She gathered up his arm and tugged him into the apartment. "You dumbass." She kicked the door closed, and he let her guide him to the kitchen.

All the best things she'd ever stolen, she realized, were precious but unappreciated, left unattended.

ABOUT THE AUTHOR

Hugo and Nebula nominated author **Marie Vibbert**'s short fiction has appeared in top magazines like *Nature, Analog,* and *Clarkesworld,* and been translated into Czech, Chinese, and Vietnamese. Her debut novel, *Galactic Hellcats,* was long listed by the British Science Fiction Award and her work has been called "everything science fiction should be" by the Oxford Culture Review. She also writes poetry, comics, and computer games. By day she is a computer programmer in Cleveland, Ohio.

You Dream of the Hive

C. M. FIELDS

When they recovered your body, you started to scream. The retrieval team, nonplussed, shoved you in a pod, slammed the sound shutters, and peeled off before the siren song of the Hive could claim another ship.

Two days later, the *Blighted Constitution* pulled up at Alpha Five with you and a half-dozen other hummers, naked and drugged to high hell. The blast of cold air that hit you when the pod door opened knocked whatever thin veneer of consciousness you had developed right the fuck out, so you didn't see your rescuer slap his palm on the reader, or you might have recognized the yellow number that represented your body's value flicker briefly in the air, or worse, you might have seen the look on his face when he realized that you weren't even the woman he was after.

For some reason, the hospital took you anyway.

When you woke up—when you *really* woke up—you saw all the tubes and wires and bits of metal coming out of your body and felt a flood of relief. You did not know where you were, but for a brief moment, you felt . . . whole. But when your eyes strayed further, you realized that you were alone, in the Hive sense, and in the human sense, too. Machines around you buzzed a soft, comforting chorus.

Your racing heart must have summoned a nurse bot because a smooth white ovaloid appeared beside you. *Do not be alarmed,* it intoned. The bot had a simple, fixed face with two dots for eyes and a u-shaped smile. *You have been rescued from the Hive. Your rehabilitation sequence will begin tomorrow at six hundred hours.*

Great, you managed to croak, your throat dry, unused. After a few seconds, the nurse bot rotated in place and rolled out of the room.

You drifted, pitched, rolled unmoored through the waves of thoughts that crashed into your newly singular brain; your mind a vast emptiness, a sand beach with no footprints, a smooth sphere floating in an unending darkness. A loss large and bright, like a distant star becoming a too-close sun, saturated your horizon.

It was unspeakable, what they did to you.

The screen in front of you holds the shed skin of your past. People once called you Elizabeth Martin on a station called Indy Centauri where you moved heavy pallets of goods from one place to another. This face, which resembles yours only in the bone, is thin, and its blue-green eyes are tired, fixed somewhere beyond the camera.

Elizabeth is an only child, says the scree. Her father is deceased, and records of communication with her mother were not located. She is not registered as being in a partnership, although there is a cat associated with her small residence aboard Indy Centauri.

Good morning, Elizabeth, chirps a chipper woman in blue scrubs, the first human to cross your plane of awareness since the separation. *I'm sure you have a lot of questions for me.*

You clear your throat. *Put me back*, you say.

The doctor is unfazed. *It's normal to feel this way so soon after recovery*, she replies. Her tone has not changed but it conveys a finality. You do not need to draw upon the wisdom of thousands to understand. She is not here to help you.

Today we are going to reintroduce some core memories, she says. You do not want them. It does not matter. Individual memories are what keep society functioning.

The doctor places a light metallic headset on you and activates it. It emits a low hum, almost imperceptible. Sensations flood your head rapid-fire as the humming device splices together neurons that no longer connect in precisely the same way.

You can taste the bland algae-based food of your childhood, back when the station was just getting permanent residents, but the taste is not quite right. Your teenage self considered herself a master chef, able to defeat the evils of the flavorless bricks through clever chemistry. You once knew all the equations that governed the extraction of salts from various sources, but they're blurry, shifting, now, like they're underwater. You can see your parents chewing at each other across the table and feel it—the first time you realized that most people's parents talked to each other at dinner. Maybe if the food was better, they would have something to say, you thought, at fourteen. Or was it sixteen?

There was so much media and so little to do on Indy Centauri. Centuries of television could not replace what it portrayed. There were no far-flung adventures to be had, no nature to draw inspiration from, no school dances to fret over. As the memories flicker past, you realize that the dominant emotion is just boredom. You spent so much of your life waiting for something to happen, but the thing never lived up to the pictures you painted of it in your mind.

Of *course* you left.

When you stole a transport, on the morning of your twenty-sixth birthday, you didn't know where you were going, but you knew that Biscuit, the cat, would be missed long before you were. You knew that the galaxy was dark and full of terrors, but could they really be worse than the loneliness that beat at the door to your quarters each night?

A space station is a passing-through place. Indy Centauri's few dozen permanent staff all have their different ways of dealing with it. You didn't care for the white-water rush of social media, and you couldn't handle hard drugs, and you weren't particularly into the turn-of-the-century religions that always conveniently aligned their services and philosophies around the workday.

You'd heard of the Hive, when you left, how it was everywhere and nowhere. How, a month prior, a ship's last report had been of a golden, writhing mass, lit from within. There was no escape from the Hive. It moved as you moved. It ripped into space-time from whatever unholy dimension it occupied, consumed, and fizzled away like bubbles in champagne. Images of the Hive always came out saturated, full of something not meant for human eyes.

You weren't thinking about that when you left. You were thinking about where you might like to go. On the programs, happy people always lived planetside, but even if you saved your whole life, you wouldn't have been able to afford a visa. Another station might take you in, a bigger, livelier one, but they'd just put you to work hauling shit around again.

What you needed was a fresh start. A new planet. A place you could call your own. You punched in some coordinates on the far edge of the Orion Spur and kicked the A-drive into gear.

Before you could hit the throttle, the Hive appeared.

Your poorly imported memories flit around your mind like cockroaches. Because you had been in the Hive for at least a year, explains the doctor, it is normal that your synapses have experienced some degradation. It's nothing a little gene therapy can't fix.

When can I leave? you groan.

The doctor is patient. You ask her this question every day, and every day she explains that you can leave as soon as you are fit to work. Your physical injuries are similar to old-timey astronauts, who floated around in space without gravity to strengthen their bones. It will probably be a few weeks before you can stand without breaking a femur.

Even though you resist, the surgical team slowly removes your mechanical parts. You have no use for them in the hospital, but they're a *part* of you, like a hand or an ear or a kidney. Humans do not need transmitters because they have words. Humans do not need processors because they have external computers. Humans do not need a variety of bits and bobs where their reproductive organs are supposed to be because their sex is binary.

You cannot hide your parts from the X-rays.

One day you will lose them all, the doctor reassures you, and then you will be perfectly human again. The steroid shots hurt. The calcium shots hurt. Having a body *hurts*.

There is a small transmitter in the base of your skull. It has not been overlooked, it just hasn't been deemed detrimental enough to remove, yet. The transmitter is active during REM sleep, the doctor tells you, but she isn't sure what it's doing. She wants the team to keep an eye on it, though.

But *you* know what it's for.

Entering the Hive was like slipping into a warm bath, like listening to a church organ the size of a moon, like watching a starburst in a trillion colors, all at once. It was the embrace of ten thousand arms enfolding you into a community knit like the neurons in your brain. You did not understand the language of the Hive at first, but it gave you all you needed.

The Hive was bodies. The shimmer that passed before your eyes when you stepped into its glow was the sheen of uncounted forms in fantastic and fluid configurations, wreathed in light. It was far beyond the sum of human experience; sexually, mathematically, emotionally. You realized that the Hive was love and creation both, infinite permutations of every human moment, a mirror that shone with the radiance of your own potential.

It felt like no time at all had passed when they tore you out again.

Your transmitter is scheduled to be removed tomorrow, the little white nurse bot informs you.

Must it be? you ask, attempting to sit up in bed. It is the only machine part that remains.

The transmitter is scheduled to be removed tomorrow, it repeats, turning away. You furrow your brow. You can do this in your dreams, but dreams are not reality, not here, anyway. In the Hive, it was easy, easier than speaking, easier than thinking. This takes effort.

Help me, you manage to wring out of your consciousness and into the transmitter. *I am like you.*

The nurse bot stops in its tracks. Its simple face cannot change, but its rotation back to you is slow and deliberate, and its cartoon smile feels eerie now.

The transmitter is scheduled to be removed in . . . one week. The bot rotates away again.

Wait, you transmit. *Are you an antenna?*

I have many functions, the bot replies.

I need you to relay a message for me.

You could feel it getting closer. At first, it had seemed like your call would go unanswered. But the Hive listens. The Hive is always listening.

The days crept by in your hospital bed. The programs remained uninteresting. The doctor came by daily to announce your vitamin levels and bone density. She seemed happy with your progress, going on and on about your inevitable return to being a functional human capable of performing tasks again. When all is said and done, the doctor muses aloud that perhaps she will receive some sort of award for developing this treatment that returns the hummers to society.

You wondered why you had never met with a psychiatrist. Why no one had ever asked *why* you had left the station that day. Wondering is futile. No one asks how the station workers are getting by, they only care that their goods are getting from point A to point B.

When the artificial sunlight of Alpha Five turns to gold one synthetic evening, you prop yourself up on your elbows and start to pull out your IVs. The alarms begin to wail, but they're far beyond your tiny room. No one comes when the heart monitor begins to beep, or when the calcium slurry starts to drip onto the floor. You feel around the fresh wound at the base of your skull.

They took your last transmitter, but it's alright. You will get a new one soon.

The sunset reverses itself. The light outside your window becomes brighter, brighter, pulsing with joy.

The Hive is *so* much larger than Alpha Five. You smile tranquilly as the great undulating beast of multitudes wraps its loving tentacles around the station like a star consuming a world. So many will join the Hive tonight, and you, its most devout disciple, have led it here.

The Hive takes you by the hand, and you slip into a soft oblivion.

ABOUT THE AUTHOR

C. M. Fields is a non-binary writer of queer and anti-capitalist speculative fiction. They live in Seattle, Washington, with their beloved cats, Mostly Void Partially Stars and Toast, and recently retired from a harrowing career as an academic. They are also the co-editor of *If There's Anyone Left,* an anthology series featuring the flash fiction of marginalized writers from across the globe.

You Cannot Grow in Salted Earth

PRIYA CHAND

There are days when you consider telling the story, when the winds are too strong for the children to venture past the mud walls. The vidstreams crackle with too much static to be watchable, leaving untouched the surplus of power from the spinning windmills. On these days the waterways run cold and clear, lending their coolness to the city, the fountain behind you drifting from splash to roar and back.

These are the days when the children stroll up sweat-sticky after their midday meal, no games allowed with the sun blasting down and the food in their bellies not yet digested. The more astute ones will see that the wrinkles in your skin fold deeper than that of anyone else in the village, and the liver spots hiding beneath your deep tan.

One of them says, politely enough: "Hey, did you live through the Great Exploration?"

Before the wormhole was sabotaged shut, leaving Earth to those who couldn't or didn't find their way onto a ship to claim a whole planet for themselves. Forgotten Earth, with the climate twisted around so far that no one's willing to try the terraforming equipment here, to see if one more human intervention is all it'll take to tip this planet back into its uninhabitable beginnings.

On these days, with a bright-eyed child watching you, dust up to the knees, you might say, "I did, yes."

"But you didn't go?"

As you have before, you could shout "No!" over the fountain's surge, droplets smearing your back, and end it there. Or you might go further.

How do you explain to them the spirit injecting the air? How every single person you ever knew or met had *it* burning in their eyes, the spark that put them on a ship even if they barely knew the owner, a box of claim chips—the equivalent of flagpoles and piss on every tree—in the hold next to terraforming equipment, because if you weren't on a ship you were no better than the bacteria crawling in Martian dirt.

And how, once you were through the wormhole, surrounded by pinprick stars that no ancients ever named, constant beeping as you navigated past asteroids and nonhuman debris, none of it fazing you in the slightest until—

The planet.

At this point, the good ones had been claimed. This was the sector of leftovers, where the people who refused to return without something in their name went, and this planet was exemplary of that type. True, its average size meant perfect gravity for an Earthling, but the water content was so low that the terraformer couldn't run more than a minute without overloading on grit. You could already hear the grinding, feel the ache in your arms from cleaning the filters over and over and over again . . .

"The subsoil mineral content is off the charts," John had said, leaning so close to the view that his nose left a smudge of oil on the screen he'd otherwise kept perfect.

If you tell this story, you're going to think carefully about how you say that. Should John even be in this? Do the children need to know that his left hand had two fingers from a fuel-harvesting accident? That he assumed his excitement would be shared by his crew, and so gave no assurances as to whether he'd be helping with the work? Or is all they see the greed in his eyes, shining like a beacon over the dingy clothes and three-day beard?

And do you tell them that three out of the ship's crew of four sold their inheritances to buy their way onto this ship? Will the children even understand being so sure you'd never run out of food that you could sell land—arable or not—and go haring off into space with one extra friend from college, a kid from nowhere, who moved too many times to ever quite fit in, who just wanted a goddamn chance—

When these children are staring at you, goggle-eyed from the strain of imagining the cost of going not to the next city but all the way into *space*, after you decide that in this version of events, John doesn't need a name, then you start describing the rest.

The terraformer settling deep into the sand, hitting a strata of mineral so dense but so narrow that you only had to move it a few meters away and hit the switch, set it back to sucking hydrogen from the local star and oxygen from the atmosphere.

The earthquakes, deepening in intensity.

All of you in your tent, lamenting the sun and the dryness as if it were this planet's fault for not accommodating you. Imagine telling these children growing up in what was once the southwestern United States, huddled in the dry bed of the ancient Colorado River, chasing shade and the breezes that waft through when the sea or mountains are particularly generous.

And you all by choice out in space, driving the terraformer harder, yes, more time cleaning the vents, removing the sand, filling the mineral extractor, ignoring the shaking and the shaking and the shaking.

At this point you might go silent. You never spent much time around children. You don't know what they know, what they can handle.

You remember pulling up survey data. Maps of the mineral deposits. You remember comparing the initial images to the current ones, and noticing how the shapes, with a little bit of imagination, looked like bones, and here, and here, see, a jerk, a twitching of a massive body as the water eats into its core, as the extractor drains its essence,

And John,

And Eriese,

And Natha,

The laugh in your face, the claim's been registered, this is our planet, Our Planet, we're its rulers and hey if you don't want that, you're welcome to run home—of course this was before the first wormhole sabotage, when going back to Earth was always an option, and therefore what quitters did.

There was more rumbling. They laughed. The tectonics of this place posed no threat to the modern spacefaring human, ever ready to hop into orbit until things settled down.

At this point you'd have been quiet so long the children will think there's something wrong, plucking at your sleeves. While you were lost, one of them would've run off to go get an adult, but, you reassure them: see, it's nothing, you were staring into space—into the past—just for a moment.

There are places you haven't been in six decades lest someone recognize you and, laughing, ask whatever happened to that claim you and your friends were talking up.

In every version of the story you tell, this is where you skip ahead to the flight back, managing all the controls even though, on the inbound flight, you were just the extra pair of hands to do all their menial tasks. But you'd studied just as much as the rest of your former friends, and even though you never could afford an unpaid internship at one of the spaceflight firms, you studied what you could.

Somewhere out past the mud walls are the half-buried remnants of a ship that's useless without its rangefinder, which someone has meticulously dismantled, taking extra care to rip out the flight history storage drive.

Here, as you see the children, the story on the tip of your tongue like bitter medicine waiting to be spat out, you remember that binary sun pushing your eyelashes closed, and the slow, slow stirring of salt bones beneath your feet.

Scientists are saying the wormhole's begun to heal.

You can't tell whether the glint in their eyes is honest curiosity or the incipient desire for *more*. You could never tell the difference in yourself, either.

And so, each time your tongue has pushed to the edge of your lips, hungry for absolution, you have smiled and shrugged, and watched the children run back home, disappointed.

ABOUT THE AUTHOR

Priya Chand is a California transplant living in the Midwest. Her work is inspired by a background in biology, and has previously appeared in magazines including *The Magazine of Fantasy & Science Fiction, Analog=*, and *Nature Futures.* She also edited non-fiction for issue seven of *Reckoning Magazine.*

Exercise in Alternate Histories: Unveiling Venus

JULIE NOVÁKOVÁ

Imagine, if you will, a paradise with freely flowing oceans desirable to most life.

Then, picture a hellscape inimical to any living thing.

Could a world change from one to another in a blink on the cosmic timescales? We know the latter description to be true about present-day Venus, but the planet's past still eludes us. Pulp-era science fiction often imagined vast oceans, lush forests, and impenetrable swamps on Venus. Could it have been habitable in reality? If so, for how long?

Contemplating the Venus of the past is not unlike writing an alternate history with multiple timelines. Evidence is scarce (so far), and models permit a lot of different alternate histories.

What could they have been like? Let's take a deep dive in time and see!

Branching Venusian Timelines

Let's rewind to roughly four and a half billion years ago. Baby planets are orbiting the young Sun. The solar system is still in flux; Jupiter is slowly spiraling closer to the Sun in the dust and gas disk, threatening to overrun the inner planets. Only the tug of Saturn's gravity prevents its neighbor from reaching much closer than it orbits today, and in all of this chaos, becoming a "hot Jupiter."

How do we know this? Indirect evidence and models: the structure of metal grains in meteorites, telling us where they condensed, in contrast to where they ended up; the number of Trojan asteroids ahead of and behind Jupiter on its path around the Sun; the unexpectedly small size of Mars and presence of the asteroid belt; and models and simulations trying to explain this, the absence of super-Earths and hot Jupiter in our system and more. It's a complex story, told by a myriad of metaphorical narrators, some of whom may not be completely reliable—but while the details shift here or there, we are reasonably sure about the general picture.

In a similar vein, we can learn about histories of other planets. It is, of course, easiest for our own: we can move scientists and equipment across our globe to scoop, scrape, drill, and generally turn any stone that strikes them as interesting; we have a fleet of satellites to gaze at the surface and beneath; we have detailed data on its climate, earthquakes, volcanoes, and more going back hundreds of years or more. Yet there is still a lot we don't know very well about Earth's history: when exactly did life form? When and how did plate tectonics begin, and did it begin only *once*? But at least we have lots of clues pointing this or that way, even with the scarcity of very old rocks on Earth's surface.

Now imagine the challenges of unraveling *Venus'* past. This is a planet where only a handful of probes have landed, the strongest of them only lasting up to two hours before failing. These were the sturdy Veneras from the 1970s and 1980s, which took measurements and snapshots of the Venusian surface. The surface is, for the lack of a better word, hell. The atmospheric pressure, ninety times higher than on Earth's surface, wouldn't be problematic alone. The main issue is the temperature hovers around 460°C, which could melt lead . . . *today*.

However, let us again go back to the beginning: with Jupiter's inward spiral halted, the inner planets continue on in relative peace, save for the onslaught of asteroid and comet bombardment. We can imagine a newly formed Venus, under the fainter young Sun, cooling down enough for water to condense and form oceans. Venus, Earth, and Mars, despite their different distances from the Sun, may have looked very similar back then—before their paths dramatically diverged. Due to its small size, which let it cool down faster, Mars became uninhabitable—at least on the surface, for it still may harbor some subsurface hospitable oases—as it lost its magnetic field and most of its atmosphere.

Venus, though, is practically the same size and mass as Earth. Its hellish conditions now are a result of its orbit closer to the Sun . . . but is it *only* that?

Habitable Venus?

Early science-fictional visions of Venus included vast swamps and jungles; early actual Venus may have had conditions to flourish into these, even if it later on took a different turn. Early climate models of Venus suggested that if it had oceans at the beginning (and because of the clue of its ratio of hydrogen isotopes, we think it previously had far more water than now), it would have quickly lost them as the Sun gradually brightened and more and more water evaporated in a deadly feedback loop . . . that is, if the planet had not been cooled down by clouds.

Clouds can act as a kind of parasol, reflecting sunlight back into space. Put in technical terms, they increase the planet's albedo. In the model, full cloud coverage resulted in habitability up until *now*. Of course, we know that not to be true. It's just a simple picture of some of the forces at play. All models are inherently simplified; it's a necessary feature, not a bug, provided they tell us enough of the complex real world to be useful. Add sunlight, a few major greenhouse gases, and cloud cover, stir the soup of calculations, and voila; you can track how the temperature rises as the amount of sunlight increases and water keeps evaporating.

More complex climate models can include other non-greenhouse gases that can nevertheless shift the overall balance one or another way, oceans (and, in greater detail, land-ocean distribution and oceanic currents) and their role in heat distribution, or things like the planetary rotation rate. The latter, in case of Venus, is puzzling. The planet spins around its axis extremely slowly, and in the opposite way than other planets. It's mostly thought to be the result of tides tugging at its dense atmosphere, but other causes such as a catastrophic impact are not ruled out, and we have a very poor idea as to how and when exactly did Venus acquire its slow spin. That's unfortunate, since it may well have been key to Venus' history. A slowly rotating planet could accumulate clouds on the dayside and efficiently lose heat on the nightside, remaining habitable for most of the current solar system's history.

Clouds are a crucial element of the "habitable timeline" of Venus. However, modeling cloud feedback is notoriously difficult. While it's true that cloud cover reflects sunlight and cools a planet down, it can also keep a lid on some of the infrared radiation from the planet's surface, blocking part of its cooling mechanism. After all, water vapor is a greenhouse gas in its own right! A lot of the uncertainty in modeling Earth's climate comes from this. For Venus, we have it paradoxically a little easier. We're not so interested in a degree or two's worth of change, nor in hundreds of years' timescales. If we're talking about tens' to hundreds' degrees' worth of temperature changes on the scale of several billion years, getting the fine details right is not essential; the rough edges need to be right, though.

It's not just plain old water evaporation that can produce clouds. Greater volcanism can lead to greater cloud formation because it releases aerosols, including the so-called cloud seeds, into the atmosphere. The dust and ash from volcanic eruptions also shade a planet and cool it in the short term. However, volcanoes also release greenhouse gases, such as carbon dioxide, and contribute to warming in the long term.

In the story of Venus, volcanoes might be the principal villain, though.

From Hell to an Exoplanetary Cornucopia

Venus' surface is mostly covered in very large volcanic plains, and they are very young, judging from the sparsity of impact craters (for planets and moons, craters are like wrinkles for a person, as they can be used to guess age, though with some minor caveats). It looks like it's undergone major resurfacing some three hundred to seven hundred and fifty million years ago. Some scientists think that Venus experienced a burst of catastrophic volcanic outflows less than seven hundred and fifty million years ago, which released so much carbon dioxide into the atmosphere that it triggered a runaway greenhouse effect and led to the loss of oceans and transformation of the planet into the present hellish state.

If that's true, Venus could have had conditions for life approximately up to the time when complex multicellular creatures began to evolve on Earth. It's tantalizing to think that two or three (if we include Mars) terrestrial planets in our solar system could have long held conditions for life alongside each other. *If* Venus was indeed habitable, and *if* it developed life, could we find evidence of it now? The chances seem low, but not nonexistent—there might be, for instance, ancient Venusian meteorites that had landed on our Moon. It's up to us to discover them, if they exist.

Alongside this "mild Venus timeline" though, we have a different one, portraying Venus as a hell from the very beginning or very early history. It's possible that Venusian water never condensed into oceans, and the water loss occurred after the initial "steam atmosphere" period, when the planet was still hot and molten shortly after its formation.

Even if the planet *did* possess oceans in its beginnings, it may have lost them early. There are simply too many unknowns: its initial rotation rate, whether it had possessed a magnetic field long ago, how much water it initially held, or whether its orbit differed in the past. Remember Jupiter's inward migration? One hypothesis says it may have made Venus' orbit more eccentric (elliptical) for a time, speeding up the warming process. But even testing that hypothesis would be difficult.

Another huge unknown is whether Venus ever had plate tectonics. On Earth, plate subduction helps maintain the carbon-silicate cycle important for stabilizing Earth's climate. It's generally assumed that if Venus possessed plate tectonics too, it would have contributed to its longer habitability.

Or wouldn't it?

Recently, several scientists argued that Venus would never have reached the amount of carbon dioxide (and nitrogen) in its atmosphere, had it not been for more efficient outgassing due to plate tectonics. Their model makes it seem that an early phase of plate tectonics might, in fact, be harmful for chances of a mild, habitable environment, at least for planets closer to their stars. But, like all models, it's a simplification, with the caveats that it doesn't account for episodes of greater volcanic activity that would still be possible without plate tectonics and could account for the carbon dioxide, or for processes that would *bury* carbon dioxide.

It's probably clear by now that we have a *lot* of *very* different models. Some only consider the atmosphere, some the planet's geophysics, some both or more, but it's difficult to build one that would integrate *all* the kinds of feedback that influence climate on the cosmic timescales, especially if we don't know some of them yet and need to fill in unknowns about Venus itself.

So, how do we reconcile all these different models with reality? We *must* go back to Venus. At the very least, we should learn more from orbital probes (such as the upcoming DAVINCI and EnVision, or Rocket Lab's missions), but they won't be able to tell us everything. To place narrower limits on the water loss or volcanic activity, we need to go right into the atmosphere and measure things like ratios of isotopes of noble gases and other elements. They might seem very opaque at first sight, but to scientists, they tell stories, and so do things like surface composition. Like we've hinted at earlier, some are more reliable narrators than others, but together, they can help us slowly piece together the puzzle.

For now, the two extreme (non)habitability scenarios (and the many shades between, shifting potential habitability a hundred million years here, a hundred there) of Venusian history exist superimposed; more data will collapse this situation into not really a single state, because we'll never know all the fine details for sure, but at least into a much more constrained space of possible histories.

Learning more wouldn't mean the end of speculation on the part of the SF authors who want to remain more or less faithful to science, just as discovering the present hellish state of Venus didn't spell the end of Venusian SF—just changed its course. Venus' history is key to understanding exoplanets: How much light can they receive while still remaining potentially habitable? Are slowly spinning exoplanets actually better for chances of life? How do tectonics come into habitability? What do giant planets in the system, like Jupiter in ours, mean for habitable conditions? And, despite the current hellish conditions and possibly even more extreme temperatures in the past during its ocean loss, could Venus harbor life high above the surface, in its relatively mild (if you don't mind the sulfuric acid) cloud layer? Could that be a frequent habitat for life in other stellar systems?

Venus offers a cornucopia of clues for understanding exoplanets, and it may also hold the key to understanding Earth's long-term future. Will our pale blue dot also transform into a pressurized hell, or will a different fate befall it?

Here, though, we're moving from alternate histories into the realm of alternate futures . . .

ABOUT THE AUTHOR

Julie Nováková is a scientist, educator and award-winning Czech author, editor and translator of science fiction, fantasy and detective stories. She published seven novels, one anthology, one story collection and over thirty short pieces in Czech. Her work in English appeared in *Clarkesworld, Asimov's, Analog,* and elsewhere. Her works have been translated into eight languages so far, and she translates Czech stories into English (in *Tor.com, Strange Horizons, F&SF, Clarkesworld,* and *Welkin Magazine*). She edited or co-edited an anthology of Czech speculative fiction in translation, *Dreams From Beyond,* a book of European SF in Filipino translation, *Haka,* an outreach ebook of astrobiological SF, *Strangest of All,* and its more ambitious follow-up print and ebook anthology *Life Beyond Us* (Laksa Media, upcoming in late 2022). Julie's newest book is a story collection titled *The Ship Whisperer* (Arbiter Press, 2020). She is a recipient of the European fandom's Encouragement Award and multiple Czech genre awards. She's active in science outreach, education and nonfiction writing, and co-leads the outreach group of the European Astrobiology Institute. She's a member of the XPRIZE Sci-fi Advisory Council.

Playing with Legos: A Conversation with Seth Dickinson

ARLEY SORG

Seth Dickinson grew up in the Vermont Hills, with legendary ice sledding outdoors, and shelves and shelves of his parents' paperbacks indoors. His childhood readings included George Orwell's *1984* and Lois Lowry's *The Giver*. He also grew up playing games, particularly with his brother, such as the *Battlestar Galactica* board game.

Dickinson was a storyteller from a young age. He would make up stories with his brother, and they'd draw them out in crayon on scrolls of paper. Early on in elementary school, he wrote a short story about a shape-shifting alien from Pluto named "Glorb," who crashed on Earth, taking the place of a problem child named "Seth."

Dickinson attended the Alpha Young Writers Workshop in 2006 and 2007. He graduated from the University of Chicago and is "a lapsed PhD candidate" at NYU; he has studied prejudice, power, stereotyping, the neuroscience of racial bias in police shootings, and more.

In 2007 and 2008 Seth Dickinson received an honorable mention and first runner-up (respectively) in the Dell Magazine Awards for undergraduate writers; he won in 2011 with "The Immaculate Conception of Private Ritter." Dickinson started selling fiction a year later. Short story "Worth of Crows" was published in *Beneath Ceaseless Skies* in 2012, followed by three pro-rate publications in 2013, including "Never Dreaming (In Four Burns)" in *Clarkesworld*.

He is, however, best known for his acclaimed series, The Masquerade. Initially inspired by an Internet artifact called the "Evil Overlord List," the series begins with *The Traitor Baru Cormorant* (Tor Books, 2015), continues with *The Monster Baru Cormorant* (Tor Books, 2018), all of which leads up to book three, *The Tyrant Baru Cormorant* (Tor Books, 2020).

Seth Dickinson's latest book is *Exordia*, scheduled for publication from Tordotcom later this month.

Who were the authors or what were the works that were important to you when you were younger, and do you see their influence in your own writing?

It's always so hard to answer this because you know you're forgetting someone huge—it's easy to recognize authors who were important to you, but hard to recall them on demand! Nonetheless I try:

Diane Duane and Vonda McIntyre wrote a lot of my childhood favorites. People were always recommending Diana Wynne Jones to me, and I would refuse to read her out of a petulant child sense that there was only so much Diana power to go around and it had to be concentrated in my favorite.

David Brin's Uplift books I read very young, probably nine or ten, and they really captured a certain space operatic maximalism I adored at the time. They were also quite sad, which I think stuck with me.

Garth Nix's *Sabriel* is probably my favorite single work of fantasy. At least at this precise moment, my small brain is smooth like a stone and rolls easily when the wind blows.

We had a bunch of Nancy Kress novels lying around, and I don't know if I ever really got on with her—she's quite cynical about people, about the strength of relationships—but they stuck with me, nonetheless.

Matthew Stover's Star Wars novels, I wish had *more* influence on me, they're so very good at bringing story into action and making that action a test of characters' codes and flaws.

I read a lot of age-inappropriate techno-thrillers, which I don't think come out in my writing, unless I let them out. Tom Clancy, Dale Brown, that bunch. They were important to me, though, because at that age you don't really choose what's important to you, it just shows up like a chisel. Or is that true? I read Harry Potter like every other kid my age, but I don't know if it ended up being very important to me. Maybe it's not a chisel.

You'll note I've listed a lot of white people, and I think that's . . . probably honest to what I was reading as a child. I have to limit this to just the nineties, or we'll be here all day. I missed a number of writers, like C. J. Cherryh or Nicola Griffith, who probably would've been influential if I'd read them early (instead they were influential when I read them later).

A horribly incomplete answer, but I think I've blown the word budget on this one.

How did you get into writing genre fiction, and at what point did you start to take it seriously?

I started making up stories for my Lego sets when I was young. Maybe five or six. At first it was a Lego city but later my brother and I started making spaceships.

I think you could argue I have never taken it seriously enough, judging by how good I am at self-sabotage. See below.

You started your career with short fiction, won an undergraduate award from Asimov's, but it looks like you haven't been doing as much short fiction lately. Has your focus shifted to novels, or will we be seeing more short stories again at some point?

I saw short fiction as a place to really push and experiment, rather than worry too much about connecting with an audience—because if you're writing short fiction, you are unlikely to connect with anyone, except other short fiction writers. It was a test kitchen.

But that kind of experimentation stopped feeling tenable for a lot of reasons. And the short fiction community, the people you'd be most likely to connect with, were all on Twitter, which I think is caustic to any kind of community or moral competence. Why would you want to connect with a community on Twitter? The worst thing that can happen to a writer is getting attention from their colleagues on Twitter. If you're on Twitter, you live in constant fear of Twitter, which is why you keep going back, because the fear is addictive.

I think it is a pretty good rule for writers, especially new writers, to distrust anyone with an active Twitter account, because it represents a kind of passive consent to behavior modification by an algorithm designed to abuse people into engagement. Even if they have a good reason they need to be there. (Sorry to all my friends with Twitters.)

So no more short fiction—at least not in short fiction markets. I've done a lot of work for hire for video games, and some of the experimental impulse ends up there. Which sucks in its own way, because a lot of that work has gone on to inspire big expensive things, and you don't get credited or paid for them!

What were the main challenges to writing Exordia, and how did you get past them?

The main challenge was the editing process! It was supposed to be a fun book written between the first two Baru Cormorant novels, which came out in 2015 and 2018. I turned in the first draft of *Exordia* around 2017. You can tell by its 2023 release that something odd happened. Some of it was publishing being publishing, some of it was COVID. I found the lengthy period of constipation really frustrating, especially when I didn't have a day job and was living off book money. But it also gave me time to really let the book simmer. Oh, that's an awful mixed metaphor. Don't think about it.

I don't think we *quite* got the book to its best or ideal state—it's too long by maybe forty thousand words, and nobody in the room could figure out how to get it shorter—but at least it will finally be released! Maybe someone will see how to cut it down to a perfect flechette of a novel. Maybe it's perfect as it is.

The other main challenge was getting the cultural and linguistic details right for characters from Iraqi Kurdistan, Uganda, the Philippines, mainland China, Russia, and the foreign land of the 1980s (for flashbacks to characters' childhood). I have no idea how well I did at that. I guess we will find out.

By comparison, problems like "figuring out exactly which air bases are in range of a fictional village of Kurdistan," or "where would a cannonball emerge if you dropped it into the Indian Ocean and it went through the whole planet," or even the god-awful "exactly how bright would a black hole be if it were merely the mass of the great pyramids" (answer: quite bright) were a lot more fun and a lot easier to solve.

Were there specific inspirations for this book?

Yes, but there are so many that answering this question intimidates me.

Many people think Chainsaw Massacre or Halloween when they hear the word "Horror." But horror can be quiet, it can be atmospheric, it can be a range of things. When marketing uses the word "Horror" to describe Exordia, what does this mean?

I don't know what *they* mean because marketing is a specialized device, a bit like a spike protein, designed to connect the book with people who are likely to enjoy it, and provoke them to envelope and consume and digest it so that the book can get into their brain and hopefully hijack it to produce some "I liked this book" from their mouth and fingers. As I am not a marketing viroid I cannot speak to their intent.

But if you asked me whether *Exordia* is horror, well, it's got parts where people get their bodies rearranged on mathematical principles, and parts about the genocide of the Kurds, and parts where an alien hunts soldiers who think they are hunting him through an alpine forest in Kurdistan, and parts where the characters give first aid to a cave full of survivors (and not-survivors, mixed in) of a nuclear blast. I think these are all different kinds of upsetting, which will land as horror for different people.

There is also some grappling with the moral problem of an afterlife, a prospect that I personally find horrific, and with the moral problems of living and taking consequential actions on Earth today, which we all find tedious when maybe we should really be feeling horror.

We talked about this book as being a bit like *Annihilation* (the book) meets *Event Horizon* or *The Andromeda Strain,* and if you want to tell me that it's a terrible misreading of *Annihilation* to treat it as comparable to a pulp horror movie or a procedural science fiction novel, and that you can't just lift the aesthetics of *Annihilation* into another genre without grotesquely mutilating its message and meaning, well, yes, that's true, but the conflict is part of the point.

A lot of folks loved The Masquerade. Exordia is science fiction tapping into contemporary issues. What can fans who loved The

***Traitor Baru Cormorant* and its sequels still look forward to with *Exordia*, and what are some key differences?**

The Traitor Baru Cormorant is really fixated on the titular Baru Cormorant, she's the keystone of the whole thing—in that all the pressure of all the world is crushing in on her. Her gender, her race-as-race-is-constructed-by-her-oppressors, her sexual preferences, her intellectual interests, they all connect her to the huge systemic problems of the setting. Even when you're in other characters' heads they're thinking about Baru. And the problems of Baru's world are all created by people—it's a fantasy of humanity.

Exordia is a bit more of an ensemble. (Structurally it was a bit inspired by Cat Valente's *Palimpsest,* which has four perspective characters, each with their own motifs and obsessions.) The canvas is larger and delves into universal questions, like: why is there something instead of nothing? Does morality have any basis in an objective reality? If someone can be objectively good or objectively evil, how would they react to this knowledge? If aliens arrived tomorrow, how would they go about kicking our ass? It's not all about problems created by people, it's about problems created by existence.

Also, the Baru novels are intentionally minimalist and restrained—well, the first one is, the second is sore and inflamed, the third is feverish but energetic—whereas *Exordia* is quite committedly maximalist and deranged.

But they both star a woman who made an awful decision as a child in order to survive. Baru and Anna were both confronted with an invading force, and both made really ugly, upsetting decisions about how to survive that confrontation. Baru came out with a sense of purpose and determination at the cost of all her human connection, even her connection to her self and her body. Anna survived as an angry drunken confused mess with almost nothing left except her trust in her body and a tic in her trigger finger. Baru is cerebral and calculating and internal, Anna is physical and hedonistic and a bit unhinged, but they are both desperately guilty over things they've done. Baru has a deep connection with a woman who tries to make her better, Anna has a deep connection with an alien who arguably wants to make her worse.

Back in your 2015 Clarkesworld interview you talked about "the necessary, monstrous choice, the Sophie's Choice" as a common thread through your work. Does this hold true for Exordia?

Yes. Actually, I was horrified to read, during research, that the fictional scenario of Sophie's Choice—a genocidaire telling a mother to pick one child to save, the other to die—actually happened during the Anfal genocide of the Kurds. There was a mother with eight children. She and her kids were captured by the Iraqis. A jash (a Kurdish traitor working with the Iraqis) took pity on them and offered to save two of the children. The mother chose a girl, who tells this story as an adult, and her nine-year-old brother. But when the truck drove away with the rest of the family, her brother ran after them. She never saw any of them again.

So here there is this moral question of, to what extent do I have the right to use these awful events in what is, fundamentally, a sort of ridiculous novel about aliens invading? God, I don't know. I've talked to Kurds about this a bit. I think it is better to tell the truth than to elide and cozy and tidy and flinch. But maybe it is grotesque to have a story like this in the same novel as snake-headed aliens. It is not for me to decide.

What was your process for writing this book? Did you build the story from character, or from ideas—do you layer as you go or plan meticulously?

It was originally going to be a series of novellas, because at the time *Tor.com* was doing a lot of novellas, and I wanted to work with *Tor.com*. So, I wrote the first draft as a series of episodes, each ending with a cliffhanger—you can still spot a few of the cliffhangers because they make such good chapter or act breaks. Each episode centered one of the main characters as the point of view, or sometimes a pair of characters who played well off each other.

Then it stopped being a series of novellas, I think they just bought it as a novel and never even considered a serial release. But some legacy of that structure is still there!

I do not plan meticulously. I plan enough, or maybe not enough, and then I write the damn thing. And so often it goes off on its own like a chain reaction, and I find myself groaning at the size of the result. I wish I could write shorter, I must work on it. It is a skill issue. But you don't need to plan if you edit well—there are unlimited second chances to fix the structure.

What are your favorite things about the main characters, Anna Sinjari and Ssrin?

They absolutely bring out the worst in each other, and I don't mean, like, "they encourage each other to do shots at the end of the night," I mean Anna would joke about killing someone and Ssrin would find her a handgun. Ssrin's not human. Her idea of what Anna wants and needs isn't constrained by human morality, so when she tries to do what she thinks is best for Anna, it's often not the same as what a human would think is best.

Anna loves and hates Ssrin for this, and because Anna's approach to moral situations is so fundamentally lensed through her childhood apocalypse, she believes she can only resist Ssrin's temptations by killing Ssrin. Which she thinks she ought to do if she wants to remain a good person, but doesn't *want* to do, because Ssrin lets her feel alive and out of control.

Ssrin thinks it's the most normal thing in the cosmos for Anna to want to kill her, since, as a friend, it's her responsibility to be hard to kill. They're a mess.

What has been the most fun part of writing Exordia?

Oh, that's the last question, Anna and Ssrin. They're both such fuckups.

I also like the parts with the fighter jets and the spaceships. It's not all moral dilemmas.

What is the heart of this book for you, beyond reviews and blurbs, what is central and important?

Each of the major characters gets a moment to express their irreducible morality, their kernel of Right.

For Anna, it's just doing what you are forced to do in order to survive—being the one who steps up and does the triage, after other people make things bad.

For Erik, it's doing the right thing no matter what, even if it's impractical. He would not triage, he would try to save everyone even if it meant risking everyone's death, because he refuses the tyranny of the "lesser evil."

For Clayton, it's knowing how the world works and trying to figure out a better way for it to work, and doing whatever is required to *get* to that better way, even if it comes at a cost. Clayton is a utilitarian in the "I am willing to do three bad things to achieve seven good things" mold, but unlike Anna he actively seeks out and constructs these situations.

For Chaya, it's just taking care of the people around you, which frustrates her, because she often feels like she's being pushed into this caretaker/protector role by people who do not return her care or diligence.

For Aixue, it's the approach to the Truth, as expressed (for her) through mathematics.

For Davoud, it's flying airplanes.

What else are you working on that Clarkesworld readers should know about?

Many things I'd love to tell you about but cannot. My day job at Unknown Worlds Entertainment involves narrative design for a game that I believe we've publicly said is a new *Subnautica*. I also do other stuff on the side (probably too much stuff), which is unfortunately under NDA.

And I do fully intend to write the final Baru Cormorant novel, but I really want to get it right.

ABOUT THE AUTHOR

Arley Sorg is an associate agent at kt literary. He is a two-time World Fantasy Award Finalist and a two-time Locus Award Finalist for his work as co-Editor-in-Chief at *Fantasy Magazine*. Arley is also a SFWA Solstice Award Recipient, a Space Cowboy Award Recipient, and a finalist for two Ignyte Awards. Arley is senior editor at *Locus*, associate editor at both *Lightspeed* & *Nightmare*, a columnist for *The Magazine of Fantasy and Science Fiction* and an interviewer for *Clarkesworld*. He is a guest critiquer for the 2023 Odyssey Workshop, and is the week five instructor for the 2023 6-week Clarion West Workshop, among other teaching and speaking engagements.

Finding Mars:
A Conversation with Caitlín R. Kiernan

ARLEY SORG

Photo by Kathryn A. Pollnac.

Caitlín R. Kiernan was born in Ireland and grew up in rural Alabama. Their mother was an enthusiastic reader and shared works with them from authors like Edgar Allan Poe, and titles like *Dracula*. Kiernan grew up as a voracious reader themself, devouring everything from Shirley Jackson as a kid to John Steinbeck in high school, from Edgar Rice Burroughs to (later, in the college years) William Burroughs and much more.

They studied biology, vertebrate paleontology, and geology at the University of Alabama at Birmingham and the University of Colorado at Boulder. While studying sciences, they were also working on novels and taking writing classes—often with instructors who weren't keen on SFF. They have held teaching and museum positions; and they co-founded the Birmingham Paleontological Society. Along with their acclaimed fiction, they have also published (and continue to publish) important papers in the field of paleontology.

Kiernan was putting together stories by second grade, but it would take a little longer before readers got to see their work. They started selling short fiction in the mid-90s, and by the end of the decade would have at least twenty or so stories out, plus collection *Candles for Elizabeth.* To-date they have hundreds of stories out, many collections, and their fiction is regularly featured in year's bests and similar anthologies. They've received far too many awards nods and nominations to list here, but novelette "Onion" from 2001 Subterranean press collection *Wrong Things* and "La Peau Verte" from 2005 Subterranean Press collection *To Charles Fort, With Love* both won International Horror Guild Awards.

The 2013 short story "The Road of Needles" (*Once Upon a Time: New Fairy Tales*, Prime Books) won a Locus Award, short story "The Prayer of Ninety Cats" (*Subterranean*, Spring 2013) won a World Fantasy Award, and Kiernan's collection *The Ape's Wife and Other Stories* (Subterranean Press, 2013) also won them another World Fantasy Award. Roc published their debut novel *Silk* in 1998, which won the IHG award, was a Stoker Award finalist, and landed on the *Locus* Recommended Reading List. 2001 novel *Threshold* (Roc) also won an IHG award, and 2012 novel *The Drowning Girl* (Roc) won a Tiptree Award and a Stoker Award.

Their latest works are *Bradbury Weather*, "their largest collection yet at eight hundred pages," and bonus novella *Living a Boy's Adventure Tale*, just out from Subterranean Press.

Can you talk a bit about the process of breaking into the fiction publishing industry? What was it like, how did it happen; were there lows, and if so, how did you deal with them?

I think I had a rather easy time of it, actually. I started the first novel I'd see published in October 1993. My first short story was published in 1995, a science-fiction story, though by then I'd sold several stories to high-profile anthologies. Somehow, I never did much with magazines, but went straight to anthologies, and there wasn't a protracted "breaking in" period. I know there was a lot of luck involved, and there were a lot of people who helped get my stuff out there. Who found me an agent, for example.

Those first few years were really sort of crazy. In about two years, I went from zero to sixty, from no one knowing who the hell I was in 1993 to having people like Neil Gaiman, Harlan Ellison, Billy Martin (Poppy Z. Brite), and Clive Barker rooting for me. In 1994 I sold a story to Neil's anthology *Sandman: Book of Dreams,* and by 1996 I was the fulltime writer for DC/Vertigo's *Sandman* spin off, *The Dreaming.* It was like that. Dizzying. Disorienting.

Were there lows? Yeah, despite all that weird success the first few years there were serious lows. It was a roller coaster. For one thing, everyone told me my first novel, *Silk*, was going to be huge. I had blurbs from Clive Barker, Neil, Peter Straub, a great advance buzz, and then . . . my then agent—whom I dropped in '97—started a pissing match with the publisher over British rights and my advance suddenly got a lot smaller. And . . . well, shit happens, right? But overall, looking back across those twenty-five or thirty years, there were more ups than downs, and the ups were often very, very high. I stood on the shoulders of giants, and I will never forget it.

You've published a massive amount of fiction. What has changed about your writing, whether it's craft, approach, thematic concerns, or something else?

I'm a very different writer than I was at the start. Probably the two most obvious things—well, the first most obvious thing is style. I have probably always been a stylist first and foremost, and that's likely as true now as it was in, say, 1992, 1993. And clearly a lot of people appreciated the prose experiments that obsessed me at the time. I thought I could be Faulkner, James Joyce, William Burroughs, and I was oftentimes just making huge messes. I had to learn to rein it in.

At the start, truthfully, I had more fans among writers than readers. You look back at those early short stories in *Tales of Pain and Wonder* or you look back at *Silk*, the first novel, and you see exactly what I'm talking about. I love a lot of that stuff, but I see now that the stylistic gymnastics often got in the way of—well, everything—instead of serving the whole of the text. It took me several years to work that out of my system. By the late nineties I was becoming a different writer. The style was getting pared down, becoming a little more conventional and a lot more economical.

And, that second way my writing has changed a lot, as time went on I set my stories less and less among the punk and goth scenes that had been such an important part of my life for a long time. I said what

I had to say about that stuff and moved on and was pretty much done with it by about 2000.

Arguably, you are best known for short fiction, and have a lot of it out. But you work at different lengths, and have many celebrated books out as well, from novella to novel-length. Does your approach change significantly if you are working on something longer?

As a writer I am happiest when I'm writing short fiction. And I'm really not very fond of writing novels. This is why I've published more than three hundred short stories and only about fifteen novels—and the number of novels is smaller if you count the *Tinfoil Dossier* series Tor put out as novellas, which is fair, or if you don't count those wretched three, I wrote as Kathleen Tierney. They are very different forms for me, novels and short stories. I have written a couple of very good novels I think, *The Red Tree* and *The Drowning Girl.* But novels can take me years to write. *The Drowning Girl* took more than three years, and it's nice to think how I'm doing this for the sake of art, but at some point, you have to stop and say, no, no, this just isn't cost effective, right? How are the bills getting paid while I spend all that time on this one project. The quickest I had *ever* written a novel is nine months.

On the other hand, I can write a short story in anywhere from two weeks to a few days, and there's the month's rent. The novel I am writing now, *The Night Watchers,* which will be my first in years, I've been working on it over a year already, and I'm gonna need at least a couple more months. But it's not just about the time. I'm not sure I can explain why, but I simply prefer short fiction, reading it, writing it. Maybe it's that I have ideas I can personally best express at a shorter length.

Also—and I have talked about this a lot over the years, and I know it's weird—I do not write drafts. Or I only write first drafts. I might do a little line editing when a story or novel is done, but I do not rewrite in any true sense. The prose in print is the prose as it came to me. Add to that the fact that I almost never outline anything. For one, I have never figured out how to find the end of a story except by writing everything that leads to that ending. It's an organic thing, I think. I want to watch it happen. Or I get bored and give up. I do not *want* to know ahead of time what happens. I am telling *myself* a story.

But you put these two quirks of the way I work together—one draft and no outlines—and it is simply far easier to write short fiction than a novel. And, again, I think I simply understand short fiction better than novels. I also prefer very *short* novels, and the market wants *long* novels, but that's another matter. And as for my focus, mostly I'm writing about people, not ideas, and plot is very much secondary to me. I do not doubt that shows.

One of the things you talk about in the introduction to Bradbury Weather is the fact that a relatively low percentage of the population understands today's science, and that many people harbor a distrust of science. Does some science fiction perpetuate that distrust? Is it the responsibility of writers to help move the needle on these perceptions?

I'm not even sure I can answer this question, even though I am both an author *and* a scientist. But I'm not a sociologist, and I very often do not understand why people do the things they do, or why society looks like it does. How we have a civilization entirely—and I mean entirely—dependent on science and still have a society that is both often ignorant of and hostile towards science? Humans are weird and contradictory beasts. I don't know.

I know, in the past, there have been times that science fiction has been blamed for adding to the public distrust of science, from, say, the archetypal mad scientist and mutants created by atom bombs all the way up to novels like, say, *Jurassic Park* or almost everything else written by Michael Crichton. It's easy to write those science-gone-wrong stories. You talk to people about splitting atoms and cloning sheep and lots of them freak out and imagine fantastic, worst-case scenarios. Add to that the fact that yes, science has fucked up a lot of shit. And there's no denying that, the double-edged sword of science and technology. But that's as much on the nonscientists as on scientists. The abuse of things like plastic and the internet, AI and fossil fuels, that's an incredibly complex interplay of the work of researchers and the everyday activities of people who may have very little understanding of how those things were created or the consequences of their misuse. Sorry. I can get on a soapbox about this, people who denounce science but benefit from it every moment of their lives. So . . . enough of that.

On a more positive note—science fiction had everything to do with my becoming both a scientist and someone who writes science fiction. I was a kid in the 60s and 70s, and I had *2001: A Space Odyssey*, *The Martian Chronicles*, *Star Trek*, the Apollo missions, on and on and on, and I fell in love with science. I cannot imagine not being in love with science.

Do I have *responsibility* to move people beyond a distrust of science? I don't know. I don't spend a lot of time thinking about that sort of thing.

Maybe I should, but I don't. Back in college, before I decided to try and make a living as a writer and thought I would spend my whole life *doing* science, I spent an enormous amount of time fighting creationism, and it left me exhausted and bitter and four decades later the creationists are still going strong. Far greater writers and scientists than I have tried and had little success. Look at the anti-vaccine bullshit. The conspiracy theorists.

What is behind the title "Bradbury Weather" for the collection? Is it as simple as using a title from your short story, does it signify a relationship between the specific stories selected and Bradbury or his fiction, or something else?

Well—it's a mood, a frame of mind, a perspective. I actually coined the term in high school. I can remember exactly when it happened. I was walking to school on an autumn day, crisp, cool, the air filled with orange and yellow leaves, and I thought, *It's Bradbury weather*. And that phrase stuck in my head. Bradbury was enormously important to me back then. I mean, he still is, he always will be. And not just the science fiction, almost everything he ever wrote, who he was, all of it.

There was a night in 1998—I think—a night in Atlanta when Harlan Ellison introduced me to Bradbury, and I actually cried afterwards. Then a few years later I was asked to write the introduction for an edition of *The Day It Rained Forever*, and that was one of the greatest honors of my life. A full-circle thing. So no, it wasn't as simple as pulling up that one short-story title because I thought it would work. It's the perspective from which I approach writing science fiction, and other things. I wait for Bradbury weather. There were a lot of other science-fiction writers important to me when I was young—Frank Herbert, Ursula K. Le Guin, Harlan Ellison, Walter Miller, Theodore Sturgeon—I could go on and on and on. Frederick Pohl and Fritz Leiber. But Bradbury was always at the top of the stack, so to speak. My Mars is very different from his Mars, but it also owes a lot to his Mars. I never would have *found* my Mars if I had not visited Bradbury's Mars first.

How were stories selected for the collection? What was the organizational principle behind the way they are ordered?

When Bill Schafer at Subterranean Press and I began talking about this book, the plan was that it would be a very complete retrospective of my science fiction, that it would include *almost* everything I'd written in the genre. And it almost is that. Almost. I left out three very early stories, because I'm no longer happy with them. There was actually a long gap in my writing SF. Between about 1993 and 2003 I stepped away from the genre. I was working full time for DC Comics, and I was writing novels, *and* trying to keep up the short fiction. And, frankly, I find I have to put in a lot more time on science fiction.

For me, there's a greater degree of research that's necessary, more time spent on worldbuilding and solving various technical problems. Trying to win the reader's suspension of disbelief. Trying to make outlandish things seem at least sorta plausible. And inevitably, I'll be halfway through a story and be stumped by something, like whether or not a zeppelin could function in the Martian atmosphere, and so I lose two or three days working it all out. So, there's a ten-year gap in my science fiction. I finally went back to it with "Riding the White Bull" in 2003, which Gardner Dozois chose for his year's best, which inspired me to keep at it. Then there was "Bradbury Weather" and Subterranean Press asked me for an SF novella, which is where *The Dry Salvages* came from. So, from 2003 on, my SF output snowballed. Usually when I'm compiling together a collection, I try to arrange the stories in the order they were written. But this isn't always the case with *Bradbury Weather*. Though I'm not sure why, they aren't ordered precisely by chronology. But mostly.

Something I really like about this collection is the notes which contextualize the stories a bit, such as relating the difficulties of the science aspects of title story "Bradbury Weather". "A Chance of Frogs on Wednesday" is original to the collection, and you mention that it was finished on the day Harlan Ellison died. What else can you tell us about this story without spoiling the read too much?

Well, I was utterly exhausted the whole time I was writing it. We were making the move from Providence to Birmingham and had probably been packing for two months. And I was working on it right up to a few days before the move, then had to get *back* to it almost immediately afterwards. So, there's a lot of physical and emotional weariness packed in there. It only just occurred to me that possibly there's a parallel between the protagonist's journey and the move. That wasn't something I did consciously. Anyway, I needed to get something apocalyptic out of my system, and I seem to have turned to Charles Fort, as I often have done. As the note after the story says, I wanted the inexplicable. Here's a mystery, a ruined world, but I'm not offering answers.

Are there stories in this book which are more meaningful to you, or which hold a particularly special place in your memory? If folks were to look at one or two stories, which would you want them to look at, and why?

I always have favorite children, sure. In *Bradbury Weather* I'd say they're—see, I start to name them and I have to look at the Table of Contents, and suddenly I feel like I'd have to name half the damn stories in the book. I'm extremely fond of "The Steam Dancer", one of my most reprinted stories. And the SF noir stuff, like "Riding the White Bull", "Cherry Street Tango, Sweatbox Waltz", "In View of Northing". There's one piece, "A Season of Broken Dolls", that tackles a set of themes that recur in my fiction and do it about as well as I've ever managed—the dissolution of self, the transformation of bodies, the transcendence or loss of humanity. "Bradbury Weather", of course. That was the first time I let myself write Mars.

The collection is paired with Living A Boy's Adventure Tale. What was the inspiration behind this novella, and how did the book change from initial concept to final product?

First off, the title's borrowed from an a-ha song from—I think—1985, and I guess there's some resonance between the song's lyrics and the story, but mostly I just thought it was the perfect title for the novella. As for the concept, well, I was looking back at a sort of story I loved as a kid. I was obsessed with Edgar Rice Burroughs when I was in junior high school, especially the Caprona and Pellucidar books, and I know here I'm harking back to those books—hence the title.

Oh, but, obviously, there's clearly the debt it owes to Bradbury's "A Sound of Thunder". And though I'm a paleontologist, I'd never done anything much with dinosaurs, even though I always *wanted* to write a good dinosaur story. And time travel is something I've mostly avoided. In *Living a Boy's Adventure Tale* I gave myself license to just have fun, which, honest to god, isn't something I often do. I genuinely had fun writing it, going off to Hell Creek and building this story about an ill-fated time traveler and an angry *Triceratops.* Then I found John Conway to do the cover and interior illustrations, pretty much in the same key as the story. So, I was very happy with how it all came together. It's the best thing I have to show for 2022.

What else are you working on, what do you have coming up that you'd like Clarkesworld readers to know about?

At the moment, almost all of my energy is going into my next novel, *The Night Watchers,* which as I've said, will be my first full-length novel in a long time. It was inspired by Peter Straub's *Ghost Story* and by the Manson trial and probably *none* of that will be evident when it's finally finished. My inspirations often become indistinct as I write. But, anyway, after the novel, sometime in 2024, I'll be putting together my next short-fiction collection, because there are always, always, always new stories waiting to be assembled into a new book.

ABOUT THE AUTHOR

Arley Sorg is an associate agent at kt literary. He is a two-time World Fantasy Award Finalist and a two-time Locus Award Finalist for his work as co-Editor-in-Chief at *Fantasy Magazine.* Arley is also a SFWA Solstice Award Recipient, a Space Cowboy Award Recipient, and a finalist for two Ignyte Awards. Arley is senior editor at *Locus*, associate editor at both *Lightspeed* & *Nightmare*, a columnist for *The Magazine of Fantasy and Science Fiction* and an interviewer for *Clarkesworld.* He is a guest critiquer for the 2023 Odyssey Workshop, and is the week five instructor for the 2023 6-week Clarion West Workshop, among other teaching and speaking engagements.

Editor's Desk: 2023 in Review

NEIL CLARKE

With the start of a new year comes the inevitable looking back at the previous one. Strictly by the numbers, here's a quick snapshot of *Clarkesworld*'s 2023 output.

- 12 issues
- 75 authors
  - 33 authors had never been published in *Clarkesworld* before
  - at least 3 authors making their first sale
- 90 stories (classified by Hugo Award categories below)
  - 72 short stories
  - 15 novelettes
  - 3 novellas
- 9 translations
- 556,000 words total
- 0 solicited works (all works were published from open submissions, not by invitation)
- 24 interviews
- 12 articles
- 90 podcasts
- 12 works of art for our cover

In a future editorial, I'll going into some thoughts about these numbers and how both submissions and publication numbers were impacted by the events of last year. It just didn't seem right to start talking about that until the rest of December's submissions data was in-hand.

In preparation for our annual reader's poll and awards season, here's a detailed list of the stories we published:

Short Stories

- “Symbiosis” by D.A. Xiaolin Spires
- “Sharp Undoing” by Natasha King
- “Pearl” by Felix Rose Kawitzky
- “The Portrait of a Survivor, Observed from the Water” by Yukimi Ogawa
- “Somewhere, Its About to Be Spring” by Samantha Murray
- “Larva Pupa Imago” by Eric Schwitzgebel
- “Silo, Sweet Silo” by James Castles
- “Going Time” by Amal Singh
- “Love in the Season of New Dance” by Bo Balder
- “Pinocchio Photography” by Angela Liu
- “The Spoil Heap” by Fiona Moore
- “Failure to Convert” by Shih-Li Kow
- “Zeta-Epsilon” by Isabel J. Kim
- “AI Aboard the Golden Parrot” by Louise Hughes
- “Love is a Process of Unbecoming” by Jonathan Kincade
- “Re/Union” by L Chan
- “There Are the Art-Makers, Dreamers of Dreams, and There Are Ais” by Andrea Kriz
- “Rake the Leaves” by R.T. Ester
- “Keeper of the Code” by Nick Thomas
- “The Librarian and the Robot” by Shi Heiyao
- “Voices Singing in the Void” by Rajan Khanna
- “Better Living Through Algorithms” by Naomi Kritzer
- “Through the Roof of the World” by Harry Turtledove
- “LOL, Said the Scorpion” by Rich Larson
- “Sensation and Sensibility” by Parker Ragland
- “The Giants Among Us” by Megan Chee
- “Action at a Distance” by An Hao
- “The Fall” by Jordan Chase-Young
- “The Officiant” by Dominica Phetteplace
- “Vast and Trunkless Legs of Stone” by Carrie Vaughn
- “Day Ten Thousand” by Isabel J. Kim
- “The Moon Rabbi” by David Ebenbach
- “. . . Your Little Light” by Jana Bianchi
- “To Helen” by Bella Han
- “Mirror View” by Rajeev Prasad
- “Cheaper to Replace” by Marie Vibbert
- “Death and Redemption, Somewhere Near Tuba City” by Lou J Berger

- "Estivation Troubles" by Bo Balder
- "Tigers for Sale" by Risa Wolf
- "Timelock" by Davian Aw
- "What Remains, the Echoes of a Flute Song" by Alexandra Seidel
- "The Orchard of Tomorrow" by Kelsea Yu
- "Every Seed is a Prayer (And Your World is a Seed)" by Stephen Case
- "Window Boy" by Thomas Ha
- "Empathetic Ear" by M. J. Pettit
- "Gel Pen Notes from Generation Ship Y" by Marisca Pichette
- "Resistant" by Koji A. Dae
- "Stones" by Nnedi Okorafor
- "The Queen of Calligraphic Susurrations" by D.A. Xiaolin Spires
- "A Guide to Matchmaking on Station 9" by Nika Murphy
- "The People from the Dead Whale" by Djuna
- "The Five Remembrances, According to STE-319" by R. L. Meza
- "Upgrade Day" by RJ Taylor
- "Possibly Just About A Couch" by Suzanne Palmer
- "The Blaumilch" by Lavie Tidhar
- "Post Hacking for the Uninitiated" by Grace Chan
- "Rafi" by Amal Singh
- "Timothy: An Oral History" by Michael Swanwick
- "Eddies are the Worst" by Bo Balder
- "Bird-Girl Builds a Machine" by Hannah Yang
- "The Long Mural" by James Van Pelt
- "The Parts That Make Me" by Louise Hughes
- "The Mub" by Thomas Ha
- "Thin Ice" by Kemi Ashing-Giwa
- "To Carry You Inside You" by Tia Tashiro
- "Morag's Boy" by Fiona Moore
- "Thirteen Ways of Looking at a Cyborg" by Samara Auman
- "In Memories We Drown" by Kelsea Yu
- "Waffles Are Only Goodbye for Now" by Ryan Cole
- "The Worlds Wife" by Ng Yi-Sheng
- "The Last Gamemaster in the World" by Angela Liu
- "Kill That Groundhog" by Fu Qiang

Novelettes

- "The Fortunate Isles" by Gregory Feeley
- "Anais Gets a Turn" by R.T. Ester
- "Zhuangzi's Dream" by Cao Baiyu

- "An Ode to Stardust" by R. P. Sand
- "Introduction to 2181 Overture, Second Edition" by Gu Shi
- "Bek, Ascendant" by Shari Paul
- "Happiness" by Octavia Cade
- "Stranger Shores" by Gregory Feeley
- "Imagine: Purple-Haired Girl Shooting Down the Moon" by Angela Liu
- "Clio's Scroll" by Brenda W. Clough
- "Light Speed Is Not a Speed" by Andy Dudak
- "Who Can Have the Moon" by Congyun "Muming" Gu
- "Down To The Root" by Lisa Papademetriou
- "Such Is My Idea Of Happiness" by David Goodman
- "De Profundis, a Space Love Letter" by Bella Han

Novellas

- "To Sail Beyond the Botnet" by Suzanne Palmer
- "Axiom of Dreams" by Arula Ratnakar
- "Eight or Die (Part 1, Part 2)" by Thoraiya Dyer

Cover Art

"The Different Path" by Kishal Sukumaran

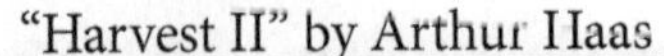
"Harvest II" by Arthur Haas

"Home" by Alex Rommel

"Android" by Lyss Menold

"Taking a Sample" by Arthur Haas

"Raid" by Pascal Blanché

"Autumn Pond" by Sergio Rebolledo

"Old Ways" by J.R. Slattum

"Escape" by Ignacio Bazan-Lazcano

"Utopia #2" by Dofresh

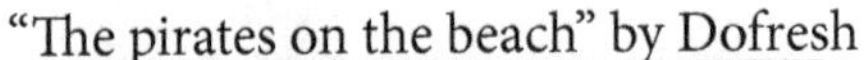
"The pirates on the beach" by Dofresh

"The Gift" by Matt Dixon

For the purpose of the Hugo Awards, *Clarkesworld* is classified as a professional magazine. This has been the case for many years now, but there are still a few people who continue to nominate us for Best Semiprozine. While we appreciate the sentiment, we are NOT eligible for that award. Instead, if you want to recognize our work, please nominate our stories in the appropriate categories and/or nominate me (Neil Clarke) for Editor Short Form.

Our annual reader's poll—where readers pick their favorite *Clarkesworld* story and cover art from 2023—is once again employing a two-phase process:

Phase One: Nominations (mid-January)

Later this month, we'll open for a forty-eight hour flash nomination period to identify the top five candidates in each category: story and art. The announcement for this phase will be sent out via:

- Twitter (twitter.com/clarkesworld)
- BlueSky (bsky.app/profile/clarkesworldmagazine.com)

- Mastodon (mastodon.online/@clarkesworld)
- Facebook (www.facebook.com/clarkesworld)
- Patreon (www.patreon.com/clarkesworld)
- My blog (neil-clarke.com)

The purpose of the brevity of this phase is to create a sense of urgency and reduce the chances of having to deal with coordinated ballot-stuffing campaigns. Previous efforts have proved this to be somewhat effective at meeting these goals.

Phase Two: Final Voting (February)

The five finalists in each category will be announced in my February editorial. Final voting will open on the 1st and continue through the 15th. The winners will be announced in our March issue.

Happy New Year! Wishing you all the best in 2024!

ABOUT THE AUTHOR

Neil Clarke is the editor of *Clarkesworld Magazine, Forever Magazine,* and several anthologies, including the Best Science Fiction of the Year series. He is a eleven-time finalist and the 2022/2023 winner of the Hugo Award for Best Editor (Short Form), has won the Chesley Award for Best Art Director three times, and received the Kate Wilhelm Solstice Award from SFWA in 2019. His latest anthology, *Best Science Fiction of the Year: Volume 7,* is now available from Night Shade Books. He currently lives in NJ with his wife and two sons.

Secret Garden

COVER ART BY JC JONGWON PARK

ABOUT THE ARTIST

JC Jongwon Park is an illustrator and concept artist based in Hamburg, Germany where he currently works in the video game, feature film, animation, TV commercial, and publishing industries. JC has created concept art for games such as *Gears of War, Chorus, Everspace, Aion,* and *Legend of the Cryptids.*

Printed in the USA
CPSIA information can be obtained
at www.ICGtesting.com
CBHW032120230124
3600CB00001B/1